He grinned—a rare sight that zapped her in the tummy and woke up those butterflies behind her ribs.

When Mac relaxed the grip on his emotions he was a sight dreams were made of. His handsome face became beyond wonderful— good-looking mixed with fun and caring and enjoyment. And sex. His green eyes reminded Kelli of spring fields, and that mouth… That mouth could be soft as cotton wool, as demanding as a hungry child, as heat-provoking as a firelighter.

She wasn't going to survive the weekend and come out sane at the other end. She was going to be in a constant state of terror in case she jumped his bones or fell under his spell and had not one, but two sensual nights in bed.

Rules, Kells. You've got rules in place.

But rules were made to be broken.

Dear Reader,

At the end of writing *Pregnant with the Boss's Baby* I wanted to write Mac and Kelli's story—so here it is.

In their backstory, they've had a close encounter of the sexual kind after their friends' wedding. Back at work they find it hard to focus on patients and not each other. So when Kelli needs a partner for her brother's wedding Mac puts his hand up—and then the fun really starts.

Weddings have become a bit of a theme for these stories, and I've loved writing them. And I haven't finished. Michael and Stephanie have been nagging me to write *their* story, and I'm not good at ignoring a good nag. So watch out for that book, which is going to come after a duet I am writing with the lovely Louisa George.

I love hearing from my readers at sue.mackay56@yahoo.com or drop by my webpage suemackay.nz.

Cheers!

Sue MacKay

FALLING FOR HER FAKE FIANCÉ

BY
SUE MacKAY

Published in Great Britain 2017
By Mills & Boon, an imprint of HarperCollins*Publishers*
1 London Bridge Street, London, SE1 9GF

© 2017 Sue MacKay

ISBN: 978-0-263-06999-0

Printed and bound in Great Britain
by CPI Antony Rowe, Chippenham, Wiltshire

Sue MacKay lives with her husband in New Zealand's beautiful Marlborough Sounds, with the water on her doorstep and the birds and the trees at her back door. It is the perfect setting to indulge her passions of entertaining friends by cooking them sumptuous meals, drinking fabulous wine, going for hill walks or kayaking around the bay—and, of course, writing stories.

Books by Sue MacKay

Mills & Boon Medical Romance

Reunited…in Paris!
A December to Remember
Breaking All Their Rules
Dr White's Baby Wish
The Army Doc's Baby Bombshell
Resisting Her Army Doc Rival
Pregnant with the Boss's Baby

Visit the Author Profile page
at millsandboon.co.uk for more titles.

CHAPTER ONE

KELLI BARNETT PULLED a face, even though her bestie at the other end of the phone couldn't see her. 'I am not going with him, stand-up citizen or not.'

'Who *are* you going to take to Billy's wedding, then? You've got to find someone pronto.' Tamara's frustration was obvious. But then her family were equally frustrated with her at the moment so the tone was overly familiar.

Her brother's wedding was turning into a nightmare. 'No one.' If only it were that easy.

'You know your mother's going to sit Jason beside you if there's no one else to take that place.'

Oh, yeah. 'Maybe I'll pull a sickie, say I've caught some severe gastro bug that I can't share with the wedding guests.' Maybe she could take a flying leap off the end of the jetty and swim all the way back to Auckland city from the island where the wedding celebrations were going to take place in less than a week's time. But no, she would never jeopardise her brother's big day.

'Are you being obtuse? Like this guy's awesome, and you don't want to admit it.'

She hated the smug laughter Tamara was indulging in. 'You've met Jason. What do you think?'

'He's doing well as a lawyer, owns his house and drives

a top-of-the-range car that goes too fast. He'll make the perfect husband for someone.'

'Not for me.'

'Just checking here. You're turning him down at every opportunity because?' Persistent was Tamara's middle name since she'd found the love of her life and thought Kelli should do the same.

Kelli snapped, 'He's dull as dishwater.'

'Doesn't light your fire, huh?'

'A wet blanket would ignite that faster.'

'And Mac Taylor would set your whole world alight.'

The phone dropped out of Kelli's suddenly lifeless fingers. 'Damn you, Tamara,' she growled, but not loud enough for the words to carry to the phone now lying on the footpath outside Auckland Central Hospital. Tam was her best friend but sometimes... Bending to pick it up, she glanced at her watch. 'Got to go,' she told Tamara in her top don't-fool-with-me voice. 'I'm going in to sign my next contract with Personnel and then get to work. Bye.' She hung up before there was any more nonsense from her pal.

But moments later the phone rang and she didn't have the heart to send the call to voicemail. 'You'd better have something sensible to say or I'll hang up again.'

Tamara just laughed. Again. 'Ask Mac to partner you to the wedding. And before you cut off our friendship for life, think about it. You two were hot for each other at my wedding. The way you danced with him said more than I know you're ever going to admit.'

Kelli jerked to a stop in the middle of the hospital entrance, yelling, 'Are you out of your mind?' She'd just spent six weeks working in Fiji on an exchange with Suva Hospital and if that hadn't put Mac on the back burner then she was in trouble. Especially now she'd been bumped from day to night shift—Mac's shift—all because another nurse had taken early maternity leave due to high blood pressure.

'Only looking out for you, Kells, like you did for me.'

Tears pricked her eyes.

Thanks, girlfriend. Appreciate it. Would love some of what you've got but it isn't going to happen. Not while I'm still afraid to reach out for it.

A quick slash across her face with her palm, a deep sniff, and, 'Why is it when someone falls in love he or she wants the same thing for everyone else?' People were bumping and nudging her as they streamed past. She was getting later by the minute. There was the meeting with Personnel—might be less complicated if she headed to the local supermarket and asked for a checkout job where she'd never see Mac—before her shift in the emergency department started at three. Very soon. It had been a full-on day, avoiding her mother and finishing unpacking from her time away.

'Because love's so good. Crazy good, wonderful. The sun shines even when it's raining. Of course I want that for you.' Tamara sang happiness.

'You think I'll get that with Mac?' She'd like to. No, she wouldn't. This was Tamara rubbing her up the wrong way causing these pointless ideas to surface. 'Don't answer that. I am not going to ask Dr Taylor to partner me to tea break, let alone anything else.'

Kelli's heart stuttered as she strode into the ED. Shoulders back, hands forced to hang loose at her sides, butterflies under her ribs.

Where was he? Looking around, she tried to calm the churning going on in her belly. Mac would be somewhere in here. He never ran late for a shift, and now that he was head of department he probably arrived extra early.

She shouldn't have come back. Doing a runner while she had the chance would've been the better option. The hospital board had sent her to Fiji to cover for a nurse coming here to upskill in emergency treatments, but no one on that board would've gone out of their way to track her down and haul her back if she'd done a bunk.

Too late, Sunshine. You're back, with another contract covering the next twelve months all signed and kicking off right now.

Where was he?

'Hello, Kelli.'

Bang. Right on cue. Slap between her ribs. That low, raspy voice raised images of a hot night in Sydney after Tamara and Conor's wedding. Without any effort or cohesive thought, she usually felt Mac on her skin, *under* her skin. But her radar must've been temporarily turned off because she hadn't noticed any change in the atmosphere until he'd spoken. Bracing herself, Kelli turned to face her heartache eye to eye. 'Hi, Mac. How's things?'

Mac was striding towards her, head up, back straight. 'Oh, you know. Same old, same old.' He shrugged as though life was a bit of a bore really. At least, she thought he was aiming for a casual movement to underline his comfort levels around her, but those muscles under his shirt were tight, tension rippling off them. 'Except it's not for you, is it? Shift change is at three, not fifteen minutes past.'

'Sorry, but I didn't ask to be bumped to the night shift,' she growled. Two could play this game. He might be setting the tone but she could just as easily keep up with the play.

His head jerked up a notch. 'I know.' A conciliatory note creeping in? Better if it didn't. Aggro would keep them apart, which was all she required of him. Unfortunately he hadn't finished. 'We had no choice but to bring you on board.' Perhaps not conciliatory, more annoyed. 'None of the other nurses would change and your return from Suva fitted in perfectly with our most experienced nurse having to take urgent leave.'

'So they told me over the phone on Friday.' Kelli didn't blame Mac for the change in her working times. Despite being Specialist in Charge his hands would've been tied, and by the looks of him he was no happier about it than she was.

'You only found out on Friday?' He sounded appalled, which won him a point or two. 'I told Personnel to get in touch with you more than a week ago.'

'You didn't think to phone me yourself?'

He swallowed hard. 'Yes. I did.'

'Yet you didn't.' Good one, Mac. Not a great start to their working relationship if he couldn't even do that. Really went to show how little he thought about those kisses.

Mac had kissed her in ways that tricked her heart into thinking he might've found her attractive in some small way. But deep down she'd known all along she was blowing in the wind. Gorgeous, sexy hunks didn't fall for her.

According to the school bullies, she had a lot in common with elephants, and not their phenomenal memories. When plastic surgeon Steve, now ex-fiancé, first came on the scene she was long past those jibes, until he offered to do breast and butt reductions free of charge.

And now there was Mac, a man who kept himself aloof from people all the time. A man who when asked if he was single by one of the nurses had replied tightly, 'Yes, I am,' and gone on with his work. His tone had been so raw no one had dared ask another thing. Yet for one night, away from home and work, sharing their closest friends' special day, he'd been different. Funny, fun, relaxed. She'd been hypnotised and felt close to him. Far too easily, considering her heart had been on lockdown since the humiliation Steve had caused her.

Which was why she and Mac had to remain totally professional on the job. She was not going through that again. Rolling her shoulders, she muttered, 'Guess we'll do our best to knock along.' And she'd do her darnedest not to remember that hot night in Sydney every time she came within breathing distance of him.

'Kelli.' Mac tapped her shoulder lightly. 'I apologise. I should've been the one to tell you about the changes, even if it was the personnel department's place to get in touch with you.'

She gave a tight smile. 'Yes, you should've. We're better than that.'

Mac scowled at her reproach, and she instantly worked to loosen the tightness in her neck and shoulders, and took a step back. No loosening the cramp in her belly while standing close to him. But keeping him onside was important. Working in Auckland Central's emergency department was her dream job and she'd do anything to keep it.

Anything? Avoid Mac as much as possible? After they'd shared kisses that had tricked her alter ego into sneaking out and letting her hair down—literally. And into having the most amazing time with a man she'd ever experienced, and that was without sex.

Her shoulders slumped. Mac had walked away when they stood outside her hotel room, key at the ready, leaving her wondering what had caused his abrupt change of mind when his desire for her had been plenty evident. A part of her had been relieved. Everything had happened so fast, those kisses so explosive, she hadn't had a moment to consider the consequences. Not least what he'd think after seeing her naked.

But since then there'd been no putting alter ego back in the box. It was up and fighting. Instead of her usual placatory persona being in charge there'd been nudges and changes going on inside that messed with her mind.

Working in Suva had given her time to take a long look at herself. Getting away from Mac and his inscrutable face after Sydney had been a priority. It had been as though he regretted their night of dancing and kissing. Which hurt bad. She hadn't been able to forget one touch, one kiss. Nor the gut-twisting moment he'd walked away from her outside her hotel room when she'd believed they were heading inside to the king-sized bed. That should've shut down all these hot, needy sensations that slammed through her whenever he came close. Should've. Didn't.

Might explain why she found it hard to return to being the woman who played safe in order to keep people on side so they couldn't find anything to pick at her about. It hadn't been about that with Mac and yet she'd still been rejected. So why wasn't she angry with him? Ignoring him? Why the heat and need for him?

In Fiji she'd figured it was time to dump the past. To stand tall and stare down anyone not accepting her as she was. To stop feeling sorry for herself and start taking some risks, get hurt maybe, loved, but most of all live. Had that night with Mac brought this on? Or was it because he'd shown her something she wanted? Excitement and maybe something more, something deeper?

Despite her new approach to life—still in training—Tamara's insane suggestion had blindsided her.

Ask Mac to partner you to Billy's wedding.

If only she could, and feel blasé about it. What if he laughed at her? Made her feel small? On the inside only; she'd never been small physically. 'Elephant, elephant.'

Those taunts had returned with a vengeance after Steve did his number on her.

So much for looking life in the eye, Kelli.

'You okay?' the man wrecking her new purpose asked.

She stared at him. 'I guess.' Her belly tightened painfully while her heart went on a rampage, beating up a storm behind her ribs. Mac was sexier than she'd remembered. How did that work? That chest stretching the top of his scrubs turned her toes upward, and made her fingers itch to slip across the expanse of warm skin covering it. That was how.

She raised her eyes to his inscrutable face, despair trickling out on a sigh. He was better looking than her brain had allowed. Definitely sexier now she'd felt his strength under her palms. A lot more serious too, if that was possible. Selective memories here. She should be thinking only of watching him walk away from her that night and the twinge of relief that nudged her, nothing else. But some things were downright impossible.

Her tongue stuck to the roof of her mouth as moisture dried up.

I can do this. I can do this. I have to do this.

The next phase of her career was going to be an absolute blast. 'Right, we'd better get on with the show. Any changes in staff since I've been away?' Apart from the nurse she was now filling in for, that was.

'Michael's swapped to our shift, having decided day shift without Conor around wasn't so much fun,' Mac told her as they began walking towards the hub of the department. 'Otherwise all's normal.'

'Cool. I like working with Michael.' Kelli looked around at the familiar territory, and tried to feel at home again. But it was impossible when Mac was within reaching distance. The Mac she'd got close to, not the Mac she'd wondered what it would be like to make love to. There was a difference between wondering and knowing. A huge, belly-tightening, heart-shaking difference, and she didn't have the answer. Her fingertips tingled with memories of him; warm skin, rippling muscles. And that was only his back, his arms. She gasped.

Stop it.

So much for putting that night behind her and getting on with her life. Kisses had never wrecked such havoc on her equilibrium before.

'Everyone likes working with Michael,' growled Mac.

Her head flipped up. Jealous? But the burnished green eyes that met hers said no, instead warning she was not special around here. Definitely not special to him. Any-where. 'I'm sure they do,' she muttered as something sharp lanced her heart. 'How did my swap from Fiji work out?'

Relief filled those thoughtful eyes. 'She was over-whelmed for the first few days but once she got the hang of the continuous stream of patients she found her stride. Talk about soaking up knowledge faster than a sponge takes in water. She thrived, and didn't want to go home at the end of her stint.'

'I can understand that.' Perhaps she could swap per-manently with the Fijian nurse.

'You didn't want to come back to Auckland?' Mac asked, his voice now grave. 'Or to ED and working on night shift?' He mightn't have asked 'Or working with me?' but the question hung between them.

She avoided the hot topic. Hot? She was standing by Mac, right? Scorching. 'Bit hard to give up those beaches and the warm water and return to Auckland in autumn.'

Did you miss me at all while I was away, Mac?

'Talked to Tamara lately?' he asked. Guess that meant no.

'Less than an hour ago.' The friend whose wedding had

started the inferno between her and Mac. 'She's sick of being pregnant, says her belly feels like it will pop open any minute.' She'd been full of unwanted advice.

'Conor told me she's as restless as a hive of bees.'

Definitely not going to talk about themselves. She could run with that. Safer, if not sad considering how well they got on in Sydney. *I missed you so much it kept me awake most nights, Mac.* But playing safe was her way and she'd grab this with both hands. Best way to put the whole caboodle behind her.

Then the phone in her pocket vibrated with an incoming text. Probably her mother, in which case she'd not even look, definitely wouldn't answer. She was not going to the wedding with Jason; nice, successful, upright citizen that he was. Today was Monday. She had until lift-off on Friday to find someone to go with her.

Ask Mac to partner you to the wedding.

Go away, Tam. *Go away.* He wouldn't want to attend a wedding where he knew no one but her.

You both only knew the bride and groom at my wedding.

Yeah, well, that was different. It had been small, and while Conor's Irish family were full on, they'd been convivial, not loaded with awkward questions about her and Mac. Unlike her mother if Mac partnered her to Billy's.

'Hey, Kelli, welcome back.' Stephanie, the head nurse on night shift, appeared before her, a genuine friendly smile lighting up her face. 'Great to have you working with us.'

Now that was a better welcome. 'Glad to be here.' Put some effort into it, 'Truly.' If not for working alongside Mac, that was. 'I'll have all those mornings to do other things.'

'Like?' Stephanie grinned. 'Sleep in?'

'More dress designing.' Her passion outside nursing. Why did her gaze slide sideways towards Mac? He was not one of her passions. He couldn't be. Dress designing. Mac. Her mind flipped back and forth. Passion.

'I'd forgotten you made those amazing dresses.' Stephanie was prattling on, oblivious to the fact Kelli was distracted by their boss. 'You ever try selling them to the fashion shops?'

Dragging her focus back to Stephanie, she nodded. 'I've sold a few that way.'

'We'd better keep you happy working with us or we'll lose you to a new career.' Stephanie reached over to the counter and picked up a file.

'Nope. Nursing's my first love. Designing's a hobby.' She held her hand out for the file. 'What've we got?'

'A lad of seven, fell off his skateboard, probable fracture of the left ulna. He's all yours.' Stephanie didn't let go of the file. 'For now I'm doing triage, but that could change. Letting you know in case you're interested.'

'Thanks.' Kelli headed for the waiting room and her first patient of the day. Of the shift, of the night roster. Of working with Mac. Her feet tripped over each other. This should be easy-peasy. It wasn't. Mac had dominated her thoughts since Sydney. Honestly? He'd started sneaking under her radar months earlier when he'd first arrived in Auckland Central's emergency department. The volume had been turned up by those kisses they'd shared, had her hormones in a right tizz.

Concentrate on work. Sure. 'Davy Roughton?' she called, scoping the room.

'That's us.' A young, distressed woman stood up and helped a boy off his seat.

Kelli crossed to them, bent down to the boy's level.

'Hello, I'm Kelli, your nurse. I hear you had an accident with your skateboard.'

His top teeth dug deep in his bottom lip as he nodded slowly. He held his left arm awkwardly against his chest. 'It went too fast.'

She grinned. 'They do that sometimes, don't they? Like they're trying to trick you into thinking you can do anything.'

Another nod, this time more relaxed. 'I can do jumps and things. But the board went over the step too fast and tipped me off.'

'You'll have to train your board to behave.' She straightened up. 'Come on. Let's get you fixed up.'

The mother said, 'The triage nurse suspects he's broken his arm.'

'We'll have Davy taken to Radiology for an X-ray to verify that. Then it will be a case of applying a cast and sending your young man home with painkillers.' She looked down at the lad. 'He's a brave soul. Not a lot of tears.'

'There were a few initially but Davy's usually fairly stoic. Like his dad.' Mum sounded closer to tears than her boy.

'Let's get this sorted. Would you like a coffee or tea? There's going to be a bit of hanging around.'

'Love a tea, thanks. Milk and one.'

Kelli ushered them into a cubicle and helped the boy up onto the bed. After settling him in comfortably she checked his temperature. 'All good there. I'll get our patient carer to make that tea, and tell the doctor you're here.'

Mac was at the bedside when she returned minutes later. 'We need an orderly to take Davy to X-ray, Nurse.'

'Yes, Doctor.' She gritted her teeth.

Since when did they go all formal? Got it. Mac was no

more comfortable with her being here than she was having to stand within metres of him, seeing, hearing him, breathing in that tantalising male scent mixed with a pine aftershave. Her blood thickened just thinking about him.

He shot her a glare. 'Now, Nurse?'

Of course. An orderly. Nothing to do with male scent and heat. Kelli phoned the orderly room, then headed to the desk for another patient file. The boy was being cared for and there were more patients needing her attention.

'Something bothering you, Kelli? You seem distracted.' Mr Distraction himself stood on the other side of the desk.

Shaking her head at him, she muttered, 'Not at all. Just getting back in the groove.' Guilt prodded at her though. She *was* concentrating more on Mac than work. After six weeks away and no contact with him, she should be over him. Her body wasn't listening, craving for more—more tender, yet igniting touches, more bone-melting kisses, more of those hands, his hard, muscular body against hers as they moved to the band's music.

'When did you get back from Fiji?' The unexpected question cut through the daydream.

'Saturday night. A tropical storm on Friday closed Suva Airport for twenty-four hours so I couldn't get out.' Couldn't drive to the airport in Nadi for the same reason.

'So you've only had a day and a half to unpack and get back into your routine?'

'More than enough.' If you didn't count the family dinner on Sunday and being pestered about going to the wedding with Jason. 'I got the groceries in, did the washing, and generally got settled. My flatmates didn't go off the rails and trash the place while I was away. It's not like I was gone for a year.' Now there was a thought. Twelve months away would take care of what ailed her. But it wouldn't solve her immediate plan of who to take to the wedding to avoid her mother's choice.

If only her family didn't worry about her so much. Sure, her engagement to Steve had been a hellish mess, sending her into a funk ever since, but now she was ready to get out in the dating world, she wanted to do it her way.

On her hip the phone vibrated. Again. Only her mother could be so persistent. Her friends didn't bother texting while she was at work, knowing she wouldn't answer. Using personal phones on duty was a no-no. Of course Mum ignored that.

Careful. Mac was watching her closely, too closely, and she didn't trust that he couldn't mind-read. He could do pretty much everything else. 'What?'

'Nothing.' He turned away.

'Good. I'll get the next patient.'

He came back, looking as though he couldn't fathom what he was about to say. 'What is it that you're not going to ask me to partner you to?'

'How—?' The floor tilted. She made a grab for the desk. Drew a breath. Tried to unscramble the words in her head. 'Has Tamara been talking to you?' Kelli knew the moment the question was out she was wrong. Tam might poke her with thoughts on Mac but she'd never go behind her back and talk to him about them. Shaking her head, she added, 'No. She hasn't. So I don't understand...'

'That was who you were talking to as you stood in the middle of the entrance causing people to duck and dive around you?' His smile was bleak. Not heart-warming at all.

At least her heart didn't think so. But she needed an answer to his question. It was none of his business, even if his name had been mentioned, but she hated hearing someone talk about her and then look away when they realised she'd heard. It started all sorts of doubts and worries.

So. Go for nonchalant. For cruisy. For this is unimportant. For my mother's already got me a date so you're off the hook.

'I need someone to go with to my brother's wedding this weekend.'

But... Come on. Add, But it's all right. I've got it sorted. The words just wouldn't form.

'You thought you'd ask me?'

No, I didn't. Tamara did. But if I'd had the courage to put myself on the line I might have. 'Just an idea. But I know you're busy, and it would be boring 'cos you won't know anyone, and weddings can be tedious unless you're involved.' Gulp. 'Sorry you overheard. It wasn't meant to be put out there. Girl talk, you know?'

'I'll accompany you.' He sounded as if he'd prefer to be pig-hunting in the mountains.

'You don't have to.' She hadn't actually asked him. Didn't want him feeling sorry for her single status. 'You haven't thought it through.'

'Are you stuck for a partner or not?'

'One of my own choosing, yes.'

'There's someone who could go with you?'

'He's not an option as far as I'm concerned.' She shuddered. Whereas this man standing before her shaking his head in bewilderment was the best option ever. Which was why she should take up the Jason offer.

Hello? Thought you'd stopped playing safe.

'Then you've got me.' Mac watched her, bewilderment giving way to amusement. 'Cutting it fine, weren't you?'

'I have been out of the country for six weeks.' *In case you hadn't noticed.*

'Don't I know it.' Shock removed the amusement. 'I mean, I… I don't know what I mean.'

Or what you want me to think you mean. He'd missed her. Not necessarily something to get excited about with that denial hanging between them. 'You can pull out. I won't rant and rave all shift.' Not aloud anyway.

'You don't know me very well, Kelli.' He leaned one delectable hip against the desk and folded his arms across that spread of chest filling his scrubs so well. 'Saturday it is, then. What time's the wedding?'

Slowly, slowly, her stomach started heading down towards her knees while her fingers began trembling. As for her brain? It was on lockdown, couldn't put the words in order, let alone utter them.

Mac's eyes were fixed on her, waiting. 'Kelli?'

Gulp. 'The wedding's at four.' As he relaxed her stomach dropped further. 'At a resort on Waiheke Island. The celebrations are taking place all weekend, starting Friday night with dinner for the two families.' She'd arranged to have Friday off months ago.

His hands gripped his crossed upper arms. 'I see.'

Ah, no, you don't. 'My parents have booked me a suite at the resort. If you're my partner…'

'I'll have to share it with you,' Mac finished for her after a hiatus in the conversation. 'You're meant to be sharing it with this other guy?' His face was bleak.

'No. He's got his own room.'

'I could get a room too.'

She shook her head. 'The resort's booked out.'

'So being in the same suite as you will make this other man believe you're not interested in him.' Then his gaze darkened. 'You're not, are you?'

CHAPTER TWO

As Kelli's face paled and her expression became stunned, Mac felt nothing but relief. He'd wager his brand-new, top-of-the-range four-wheel drive that she was not the slightest bit interested in this other man and was not using him to make the guy jealous. 'Why don't you just tell him you don't want to go with him?'

'I've tried heaps of times, but with my parents backing him he thinks I'll see I'm wrong.'

'Tricky.'

'Very.' Her face tightened, her eyes anxious. 'You won't be able to swap your Friday shift at such short notice.' Then the caution deepened. 'Will you?'

Seemed having a partner was important to Kelli. Deep despair had dulled her eyes earlier when she'd been on the phone presumably talking to Tamara. He'd been within touching distance and yet she hadn't noticed him or any of the people pushing past. It was that despair that had him offering to help her out because he'd been there, knew how hard it was to face demons alone. Not the sanest offer he'd ever made when he was meant to be trying to put distance between them, but would he retract it? No way. Even if that was where he might be headed this weekend. 'I'll pull in a favour. You going to tell me what this is about?'

Her eyes widened as she looked beyond him. 'Later,' she murmured.

'Kelli, can you meet the ambulance due any minute?' Stephanie was upon them. 'We've got an eighteen-year-old male, drowned while surfing at Piha. He was revived, but secondary drowning is now a concern. You want this one, Mac?'

No, I want a case three floors up where I don't have to see Kelli, hear her voice, or be reminded what a total pushover I've been. Partner Kelli to her brother's wedding? I can't believe I offered to do that. Talk about a stupid idea.

It wasn't as if Kelli had begged him. She'd been shocked by his offer. Mac tapped his head with a clenched hand. 'I'll see him. Michael might like to join us since secondary drowning doesn't occur every day.' Then the atmosphere around Kelli and himself would be diluted somewhat.

'I'll go tell him.'

The bell from the ambulance bay was loud in the sudden silence between him and Kelli. Then she shook her head and rushed off to collect their patient, those endless, shapely legs eating up the distance with haste.

Mac watched her go. Waited for her to return. One hour working with her and he knew he'd made a big mistake filling the vacancy with Kelli. Not that he'd had any choice. She was distraction personified, made it impossible to think logically. Hence putting his hand up for that wedding position. What other reckless suggestions would he be making after a whole shift? A week? He'd be better off spending the coming weekend at Piha Beach where he could dig a large hole in the black sand dunes and bury himself, not spending the days on Waiheke with Kelli, mixing and mingling with her family, and no doubt being given a thorough look over.

No, mate, that's not your problem. The real problem here is that hotel suite. Double beds are a given in these places.

All he could hope for was that there were two. But something deep in his gut told him what fate thought of that idea.

Two nights sharing a room with Kelli would test him beyond measure. Hell, one night dancing with her in Sydney had burned him deep. Deep enough to bring up all the walls to keep from getting close when they were outside her hotel room and the enormity of what they'd been about to do hit home. Even casual sex with Kelli would've exposed more of himself than he had since his beloved Cherie. Mac grimaced. No pun intended. He hadn't been ready to let his emotions out of the box when they were still tender and bruised. The weeks Kelli'd been in Fiji had been a relief. Had given him time to put that escapade into perspective. He'd been determined that Kelli was not going to become a part of his life outside work. Yet one hour in and already that was a total screw up.

They were going to spend a whole weekend together. All because of his big gob.

Over the past six weeks he'd missed her more than he'd believed possible. But he wasn't ready. Doubted he ever would be. Not even a short fling with no strings. Doubted Kelli was a casual fling kind of girl given the intensity she approached people, work, pretty much everything, with. Unfortunately for her, for him, he'd given his heart to Cherie, and didn't have a second one beating in his chest. Moving beyond the dark that had resided in there since—since the day his life had blown apart and grief became his norm—wasn't possible.

Yet whenever an email from Kelli had come in on the department site during the past weeks he'd read it avidly to see what she was up to. Her account of fishing far out from land in a tiny canoe with the locals had had his heart racing, even though she'd obviously returned safely. There'd been a photo of a grinning Kelli holding up a trevally she'd caught. That grin had got to him, tightened his gut and other parts of his anatomy, but, worse, it had started gnawing away as if he was missing the point somehow.

He'd wake up in the middle of the night in a cold sweat only to lie staring at the ceiling, his heart pounding while images of Kelli paraded through his skull. Kelli in that figure-defining bridesmaid dress, Kelli dancing at Tamara and Conor's wedding celebrations, Kelli strolling down Darling Harbour pier afterwards in six-inch-high green shoes as if she were in sneakers. In his arms, reminding him of what he'd lost and couldn't contemplate opening up for again. In case he...

'Mac?' Stephanie waved a hand in front of him. 'Your patient's in cubicle two.'

Truly? How had he missed the stretcher being pushed past? Was it possible that Fiji Hospital ED needed to swap out a doctor requiring to upgrade his or her skills? Could it be a twelve-month exchange? Because he was available, as of right now. 'I'll just grab Michael.'

'He's already there.'

If he didn't know better he'd believe Stephanie was laughing at him. So he didn't answer, didn't give her anything else to be amused about. Pushing through the curtain into cubicle two, he introduced himself to the young man. 'Beau, I'm Mac, a doctor. I hear you got into some trouble surfing this afternoon.'

'The ambo guy said I drowned. But that was ages ago. Why am I in here? The surf club guys brought me round.' His hands were picking at the bedcover. Grumpy and twitchy.

'Drowning's no picnic. We need to monitor you for a while. Also I want to see if there's any water still in your lungs.'

'I reckon I coughed it all up. A little bit can't hurt, can it?' The words were snapped out. Aftershock from drowning, or his normal mannerism? He did appear a little bewildered.

'Do you remember much about things before the helicopter picked you up off Piha Beach?'

'Lots of people hanging around, talking at me.'

Kelli already had the pulse oximeter on his finger to keep tabs on his oxygen saturation. She was focused on their patient.

As he should be.

'Can you sit still for me, mate?' Michael asked. 'I can't listen to your lungs while you're moving so much.'

Beau scowled but sat stiffly, only moving to breathe deep when Michael asked.

Mac explained. 'You drowned, and had to be resuscitated. We need to keep an eye on you for a while yet in case there are any complications.' Mac glanced at Kelli. 'Heart rate?'

'Sixty-nine.'

Near to normal. Moving in beside her, Mac said quietly, 'Watch for mood swings. Beau seems edgy, but that might be his personality.' He tried not to breathe in that scent of flowers, but his lungs couldn't hold out until he'd moved away. Roses. Red ones. Like the ones in his mother's garden when he was growing up. But this scent was beguiling and tempting and—unwelcome. He bit down on the groan of longing building in the back of his throat. The night ahead stretched out interminably.

A bell sounded from the ambulance bay. Relieved to have an excuse to get out of this airless cubicle, Mac turned to head away. Drawn back to Kelli, he coughed. *Let it go, man.* But he just couldn't. 'It's good to have you back. The place's been dull lately.' It had? She hadn't even worked the same shift as him until today.

'I'm not noisy.' The tone might've been sharp but her mouth twisted in that adorable way he'd begun noticing at the wedding dinner.

'I always know when you're around.' *Talking too much, Mac Taylor.* There were hours to get through yet. *And* this was only day one of three hundred and sixty-five minus weekends. All those days to get to know Kelli and maybe understand why he felt different around her, if there was some hope for his future.

Kelli's head shot up. Despair and puzzlement shone out of her cobalt eyes. A faint pink blush stained her cheeks. 'Just as well I've been away then, isn't it?'

Mac forced his mouth shut and made for the curtain again, his stomach in a knot. He didn't trust himself not to come out with something equally stupid as that last little nugget. Before she'd taken the job in Fiji he'd only ever seen her as her shift was finishing and his beginning. Yes, and he'd always noticed her. Now he'd gone and told her much the same. Didn't make sense. It wasn't as though he was interested in her outside work.

Then why had he taken her to that Sydney night club after Conor and Tamara's wedding? How could he not, when she'd been beautiful in her emerald-coloured fitted gown and those shoes that weren't made for walking? Yet Kelli had walked the length of the pier and back in them. She had to be some kind of acrobat to be able to do that without falling off the heels and breaking her long neck. A delectable, beautiful, annoying acrobat whom he'd kissed—a lot. And ever since then, he'd not been able to forget any moment of that night. Was that why he'd agreed to go to this next wedding with her? Because after the last ceremony they'd made out together, and might repeat the scenario? He needed his head read—by an expert in craziness.

Behind the curtain he heard Beau ask in a wavering voice, 'Can I phone my mum?'

'Of course,' Kelli answered. 'Here's your daypack. Will your phone be in there somewhere?'

'I hope so.' The guy suddenly sounded much younger and vulnerable.

'I'll leave you alone to call her, but I won't go far in case you're worried something might happen. Want a coffee?'

Mac made a beeline for Resus and the patient being wheeled through from the ambulance. Having Kelli find him hanging around outside the cubicle was not an option. He might feel like a seventeen-year-old in lust but for Kelli to recognise that would blow the lid on any hope of working together with some semblance of normality. As for what spending the weekend in close proximity of each other would do to him, he couldn't begin to imagine.

The paramedic greeted him with, 'Mac, this is George Falkiner, fifty-one, a digger driver. The ground gave way under his three-ton machine and he was tossed out and then hit by the bucket. He's stat one, hasn't regained consciousness in the time we've been with him. Multiple fractures to both arms and the right leg. Suspected internal injuries around the spleen and liver.'

'I'm surprised he's still breathing. Let's get him onto a bed and hooked up to our gear. On the count, everyone.' Their patient was quickly transferred from the stretcher to the bed, and Mac began an examination. 'Stephanie, I

need blood bank on the line yesterday.' The guy was losing blood from a torn artery in his groin faster than water
leaving a bath. Those internal injuries would be bleeding
too. 'Get some group O sent down and a tech to take a
crossmatch sample for further transfusions.'

'Onto it.'

'Then call Radiology.' Mac had started at the man's
skull, gently probing for crushed bones and bleeds. He
did not like the guy's chances, but that wouldn't stop him
doing everything within his power to save him. Including
putting all thoughts of Kelli aside.

Around him nurses and another doctor worked quietly
and efficiently stemming blood flows, monitoring heart
rate and blood pressure, examining limbs and probing for
other injuries. A lab tech arrived with blood and a test kit
to take a sample for blood grouping. George Falkiner had
a damned good team on his side.

The cardiac monitor emitted the flat sound of no heartbeat. Mac snatched up the paddles. 'Stand back.' With a
check that everyone had done as ordered he applied the
electric jolt needed to restart the man's heart. It worked.
'Now there's a wonder. He's lost so much blood I didn't
expect to bring him back.' But for how long? Sometimes
things worked right, and sometimes: well, Mac wasn't
going there. His patient didn't need the negative vibes.
He'd managed to score enough on his own.

Mac was completely unaware of anything going on
outside Resus. His focus was entirely on his patient, and
it wasn't until they'd finally stopped the bleeding except
for some internal strife, that he began to think there was
a chance this man might make it. Radiology took their
pictures, Theatre was on standby, and a general surgeon
and orthopaedic surgeon were up to speed on what was
required for their patient.

When George was finally wheeled away to Theatre Mac straightened his aching back and rolled his neck to loosen the muscles that were sporadically cramping. 'Glad that's over.'

'Grab a break while you can.' Michael spoke from the desk. 'The numbers are starting to crank up out in the waiting room but nothing urgent. I'll go after you get back.'

'Think I will.' A cold drink and something to eat would do wonders for the weariness gripping him now that the urgency of that case had gone. Tossing his scrubs into the laundry bin and pulling on clean ones, he headed for his office and the snack he'd put together earlier at home.

Once at his office desk he decided to stay put and do a bit of paperwork while he chewed on sandwiches. Even signing off a single document was one less to worry about. Not mentioning that in this airless pokey room he was safe from Kelli scent, Kelli comments, and definitely the wariness in those blue eyes that had appeared from the moment he'd agreed to be her partner this coming weekend.

Knock, knock. A head popped around his door. Kelli. Of course. So much for a few minutes' escape.

'Hi, everything okay?'

She stayed in the doorway. 'Just giving you the heads up. A nine-year-old girl fell ten metres off the family deck onto a fence post. Stat one. The chopper's bringing her in from Waitakere, ETA approximately ten minutes.'

Mac winced. 'Nine, eh? That's a small body to land on a solid object from that high.'

'The mother's with her.' Kelli stared at her hands. 'A parent's nightmare really.'

'How do parents cope with not always being able to keep their kids safe? It would drive me crazy.' Keeping those he loved or cared about safe was as ingrained as taking a shower every day. Not that he always did well at saving people. He looked at his bare ring finger as if he needed reminding.

'I guess they can only set the boundaries, keep a vigilant eye out, and cross their fingers.'

That didn't stop bad things happening. He'd done all of that and yet his wife had died. In bed. Beside him. While he slept. He was a doctor, and that had meant absolutely nothing when he was most needed. He should've sensed something was wrong with Cherie even in his comatose state brought on by exhaustion after too many sixteen-hour shifts in ED. But he hadn't. The aneurysm had been a silent killer, stealing the love of his life and their unborn infant.

Pushing down on the flare of pain and distress, he growled, 'Let me know when the helicopter's landed.'

'Yes, Doctor.' The door closed with a small bang.

Fair cop. It wasn't Kelli's fault he was flawed, hadn't been able to save Cherie. No, that was his to own. But it didn't give him licence to be surly with Kelli. Yet how to keep her away? How to stop the fissures she was opening within him from spreading throughout his soul just by being around her? She had hang-ups aplenty. Was always trying to appease people and keep the department happy and relaxed—except when it came to him. Then she could be lippy as all hell. Lippy. Lips. Oh, hell.

Those lips, that mouth. Soft while demanding, hot and giving, made to bring a man to his knees. How he'd walked away that night was beyond him. Showed the strength of his fear of opening up to another woman, because, as far as he could work out, that was the only reason he'd hightailed it away from her.

Hopefully his abrupt dismissal might keep her distant for the rest of the shift. By tomorrow he'd be over whatever was tying him in knots every time Kelli came near, and remember only that she was an exceptional nurse who always went the extra distance for her patients.

An attractive nurse with a body that filled scrubs in a tantalising way they weren't designed for.

A woman with shiny dark blonde hair piled on top of her head and kept in place with carefully positioned decorative combs. And when those combs came out, the thick locks had been satin in his fingers.

He wouldn't think of the smile that warmed him right down to his toes, and the laugh that lodged in his chest when he wasn't on guard.

All of that was before Sydney, buster. Not only since then.

Mac threw his pen at the far wall. Ping. Didn't underline his feelings. The water bottle followed. Bigger ping. Just as well he'd already drunk the contents.

Not feeling any better here. Cherie had been the love of his life. Had been? Still was. There wasn't room for another one. He'd never recover if something went wrong a second time. He was still recovering from losing Cherie.

Where was that chopper?

Ten minutes could whizz past in seconds, or it could drag out into an hour. Today was the drawn-out version. Mac chewed and chewed on his tasteless sandwich: cold beef with zucchini pickle care of his mother. She sent him a package about once a month, filled with jars of homemade jams and pickles, a fruit cake, and sometimes in winter homemade chocolates, which he gave to the kid next door. Comfort food that he enjoyed but wouldn't admit to in case it made him look like a spoiled brat.

His mother had been the cushion in his life growing up with a tyrannical father who believed his way was the only way for just about everything. Make that *absolutely everything.* So the packages were warmly accepted as a reminder of his mother's unconditional love and how not everyone was hard on others. They'd stopped when Mac married, but about a month after Cherie died there'd been one on the doorstep when he'd got home from work, and they hadn't stopped since.

Stephanie waltzed through the door without any pre-amble. 'Our girl's being brought down from the landing pad now.'

Instantly on his feet, Mac tossed the remainder of his snack in the bin. 'Let's go.'

'If it's okay, I've put Kelli on this one. She's good with the littlies.'

So were other nurses, and they weren't distracting. But, 'Why wouldn't it be all right?'

Stephanie watched him, her head on a slight angle. 'I think you can probably answer that better than me, but it seems she's got you rattled.'

Fortunately Stephanie headed out of the room so he didn't have to come up with some unlikely reply, denial being at the top of the list. And if he denied what she was implying, he'd be lying.

His gut had been in turmoil from the moment he'd seen Kelli on the sidewalk outside the hospital on the phone to Tamara, and didn't feel as if it intended settling down any time soon.

Time to focus on the job, starting with the young girl now arriving in ED.

Izzie had been given morphine making her barely coma-tose, which was a good thing, Mac decided as they worked to find the extent of her injuries. She'd hit the post with her thigh, fracturing the bone in three places. Her pelvis hadn't come off any better.

'Thankfully none of her organs were damaged,' Mac informed the girl's mother as they waited for the orderly to take the child to Theatre to have those bones seen to. 'Nor is there any head injury apart from the cut above her eye, though there's a severe whiplash to her neck, which will cause ongoing issues with headaches and muscle tension. Izzie will be referred to a neurologist for help with that.'

Tears poured down the young mother's face as she gripped her unconscious daughter's hand. 'But she will be all right? Won't she? Please say yes.'

He wanted to. He *really* wanted to. It was inherent in him to make people feel better, or safe, or at least able to function normally. It was something that had started the day he saw his father kicking the family dog for being sick on the kitchen floor. Mac had snatched Pippy away and run for the garden shed, only to be followed and given a lesson in not letting animals or people turn him into a miserable excuse for a man.

But being honest was right up there too. 'Izzie may always walk with a limp. Whiplash can also be hard to completely put right.'

The tears became a torrent. 'My poor little girl. It's not fair. She's always been such a monkey, climbing trees and ladders and getting into places no one would've thought possible. She terrifies me at times, but there's no stopping her. She thinks she's bulletproof.'

'She's probably had the biggest wake-up call possible.' *Or she'll take it on the chin and carry on being a monkey.* 'Parenting, eh? Who said it was easy?'

'You got kids, Doctor?'

Cherie had been four months pregnant when she died. 'No.' The word spat out, so he added with more restraint, 'Not yet.' Never. Unless… Unless he could talk about the past, undo those crippling fears enough to let the sun shine in—as in Kelli sunshine.

Right that moment Kelli walked past, helping her next patient, an elderly man with what appeared to be severe arthritis in his leg. She did not acknowledge him. Had been distant in the room with Izzie. Had been distant ever since leaving his office an hour ago.

Hopefully she'd find him a smile before the end of the week or it was going to be a long, awkward weekend on Waiheke Island. It was already a long, awkward shift.

Bring on eleven p.m.

That time did eventually tick over. Monday's were never frantic but this one seemed quieter than usual. In other ways Mac's mind was constantly on alert, Kelli alert. Her laughter, her voice, scent, the way the air cracked like an approaching storm. For eight hours he'd been put through the wringer, his body tense and filled with need. Immediately after completing handover he grabbed his bag and headed to the staff gym in the hospital basement. A hard workout would fix what ailed him.

In shorts and sleeveless sports top Mac strode into the workout room and slammed to a halt. He wasn't alone. Nothing new in that. But never before had Kelli Barnett been here at the same time. Then again, she worked night shift now. He hadn't known she worked out. Memories of firm muscles and a flat abdomen, a stunning figure accentuated by that dress, waved at him, reminding him of how his groin had tightened. Was tightening now. Went to show he hadn't really thought about it.

As he watched those long legs running on the treadmill his heart rate was increasing exponentially. Endless legs wound around his waist as they— Gulp. Out of here, now.

She hadn't seen him. He'd be gone before that changed. No way was he working out in the same room as Kelli.

'Hey, Mac, how's things?'

Spinning around, he came face to face with the surgeon who'd operated on young Izzie. 'Andrew, haven't seen you in here for a while.' *And I'm not about to, considering I'm on my way out.*

The pounding of feet on that treadmill was increasing in speed and noise. If Kelli was working up to a top speed she wouldn't be looking around the gym to see who else was here. He might still get away.

'Want to lift some weights?' Andrew asked.

'Not tonight.' He stepped aside, intent on leaving, but couldn't resist glancing across to the treadmills.

Caught. Kelli was holding onto the handlebar with one hand and staring at him as though she was oblivious to what her legs were doing. Her face a picture of surprise and—and annoyance? Either way, she definitely wasn't happy to see him.

She stumbled. Grabbed at the bar with her free hand, tried to get back to the measured, fast steps required to keep up with the machine's set speed. She kept tripping, as if she couldn't quite get it right.

Mac was already halfway to her. 'Hit the slow button,' he called as worry thickened his throat. Fall and chances were she'd twist an ankle or sprain a wrist.

The treadmill stopped. Instantly. Kelli lurched forward, banging into the control panel.

'The slow button, not the off one.' But he was too late telling her that.

Kelli remained upright, her breasts rising and falling fast, her hands at her sides. But man, could she curse.

Mac stopped beside the treadmill and watched her, his worry backing off, replaced with silent laughter as she gave herself a right lecture. 'Come on. You're not that bad,' he intervened at last.

Then she removed earplugs and glanced at him. 'Did you say something?'

'Nothing as potent as that diatribe I just heard.'

Heat seared her cheeks, turning them a sharp shade of crimson. 'Ouch. Did anyone else hear me?'

'I doubt it. You're a quiet banshee.'

'I'm stupid, is what I am. Losing focus and nearly falling flat on my backside. I can see the photos now. All dressed up for the wedding and sporting bruises up and down my thighs.'

That brought up a mental picture Mac couldn't contain. His gaze dropped to her thighs. Under Lycra they were toned, smooth, mouth-watering. The skin he could see was tanned, probably the result of time spent in the tropical sun. Then he heard the rest of her sentence. 'Is your dress very short?'

'It's ankle length.' Kelli looked away. 'With splits up both sides.'

'How high do these splits go?' He wasn't going to survive if they reached higher than her shins.

'Umm, to the top of my thighs.' She still didn't look at him.

'Oh, man.' Survival was out. His heart was already practising speed-dialling and another part of his anatomy was doing a sit-up. 'I see.' Unfortunately he could. His imagination was particularly overactive tonight. Pumping a few weights wouldn't have helped at all. He'd probably pull a muscle. *Don't go there,* his mind shouted.

'You getting on a treadmill?' his tormentor asked.

'I'll hit the rowing machine first.' Instantly he wanted to snatch the words back. What was wrong with one of the cycle machines? They weren't directly in front of the treadmills.

'Right,' Kelli muttered and punched some buttons to start the conveyor beneath her feet moving. 'Right,' a little louder as she slipped her earplugs back in place, pressed the gradient mode and began pounding uphill.

CHAPTER THREE

KELLI RAN UP and down hills on the same spot until the distance monitor came up with five kilometres.

Mac was still in front of her, sweat pouring off him as he worked those pecs and shoulder muscles, rowing his heart out.

While *her* heart was racing with exertion, and disconcerting need for the man in front of her.

She ran another two kilometres. Her legs might be getting tired, but her brain was still tripping around fast as though it had received a sugar bomb. Not lust, or desire, or anything to do with Mac. Couldn't be. Those emotions were on lockdown, afraid to surface in case she got sucked in and her heart torn out again when she was only just getting it back in shape after the last time. Now that they were spending the weekend together she had to be more vigilant about keeping hot thoughts about him under wraps. She couldn't have him looking at her and reading her emotions and needs. Nor could she deal with him kissing her senseless then turning away. Not a second time.

Did she mention desire? Hot and expanding throughout her weary body, her sluggish muscles; livening her up, not preparing her for sleep when she got home.

Time to stop the machine. Nothing was going to shut her brain up. Not in here anyway. Not with Mac wearing the sleeveless top that showed sweat-slicked, tanned skin, and muscles that reminded her how hard that body had felt under her palms.

Slowing the treadmill at a sensible pace this time, Kelli dragged in lungfuls of air and gave up trying to ignore the beautiful sight before her. Mightn't get another opportunity.

Those broad shoulders tapering down to a trim waist and flat belly made for a perfect package. That night dancing in Sydney he'd made her feel small and dainty. Enough so she'd let her hair down and enjoyed being with Mac on the dance floor, letting loose in a way that had made her briefly forget all her insecurities about her size.

'You going to stand there all night? Or are you going to do some more exercise?' Mac called over his glistening shoulder.

'You got eyes in the back of that shaggy head?' His thick, dark blond hair had lost all semblance of the usual clean-cut style, instead stuck to his scalp with small curls appearing at the edges. Cute. As in man cute, not baby cute.

'Something like that.' The rowing machine was slowing, Mac relaxing and letting his arms drop. When he stood up he scrubbed his face with his hand towel. 'I'm starving. Feel like hitting The Grafton All-Nighter for something to eat?'

Kelli would've said no, she didn't need food; but her stomach had other ideas, announcing with a loud rumble that some grub was the best idea all night. She bit back a curse. Already she doubted she'd get any sleep tonight, and spending the next hour with him would cancel tomorrow night's quota of zeds as well. 'Thanks, but I'll head home and see what's in the fridge.' Yoghurt, tomatoes, lettuce, a cucumber and a loaf of bread. Yesterday's shopping hadn't been extravagant or expansive.

'You want to avoid me?' Mac asked softly.

'Yes.'

'When I'm officially your partner for the weekend?' he added in that soft voice that lifted bumps on her skin.

'Isn't that enough?'

A spark of hurt flicked across his face.

Got that wrong, hadn't she? 'I thought it'd be enough with you meeting me on Friday and going from there. I didn't want to take up any more of your time than I'm already doing.' He hadn't exactly rushed to welcome her when she'd turned up for work that afternoon after a six-week absence, so he wasn't likely to want to hang with her much now. Yet he had volunteered for the weekend. Nothing made sense when it came to her and Mac.

His hurt remained. Who'd have known he was so sensitive? Not her. Which only added to the guilt starting to crowd her mind.

'I need to be brought up to speed on a few things,' he admonished, still softly, but there was no denying the grit behind his words. 'I can't put my foot in it when it comes to your family. They'll expect me to know something about them. Then there's the other guy.'

Fair enough. 'Five minutes for a shower?'

'You sure you're female?' Mac started to smile, then stopped. 'See you shortly.' He was off, striding across the room, putting distance between them quick fast.

Sharing a meal at The Grafton All-Nighter was going to be a *load* of fun.

'I've got Friday off,' Mac told Kelli after they'd placed orders for bacon and eggs, and lots of tea.

'That was quick.' Keen? Nah, determined, more like.

He was known for his take-no-prisoners approach to getting things done.

'It comes with having done many favours over the past year.' He sculled some water. 'What time do you intend catching the ferry to Waiheke on Friday?'

'How about four-thirty at the heliport downtown?'

His eyes widened, but all he said was, 'Fine.'

Kelli felt driven to explain. 'It's my dad's way. Ever since he became successful and the business grew so huge he's enjoyed sharing it round, feels he owes it to those who knew and helped him back in the dirt-poor days.' Her father was kind, generous to a fault, not a show-off.

'What's he in?'

'Civil engineering.'

'With the growth going on in Auckland I can see how he's done well.'

'The harder he worked, the luckier he became,' Kelli quipped, but couldn't deny her pride. 'My brothers, all three of them, work in the business. An engineer, a lawyer and an accountant slash business consultant.'

'You stepped outside the square.' Something passed through that intense gaze, something she couldn't name. Admiration? For her? Not likely. Probably a question about why she hadn't gone into the family business that he was coming up with a load of incorrect answers to.

'After growing up hearing about the company day in, day out, I wanted something different, something that was about me. Choosing a career where I could help people, make them feel better, was it.'

'We're on the same page there. Primarily I did medicine to help others. Plus being good at science and maths made it a no-brainer.' Mac leaned back in his chair, stretched those long legs to the side of the small table. 'Why is helping others so important to you?'

Eek. This was getting serious. Trying for nonchalance, she told him, 'I can't explain it. It's just who I am.' There was truth in that, possibly brought about from the hurt she'd dealt with, hurt she hoped others didn't suffer. 'I could ask the same of you.'

'I hate seeing people in pain.' Short, snappy words, with a dirty great stop sign behind them. Followed by, 'Which brother is getting married?'

Back on track, off taboo terrain. 'Billy, the engineer. His fiancé, Leanne, works in the accounts department of the firm. My other brothers are married and their wives also work there. I'm definitely the odd one out.'

'That bother you?' His mouth did that delectable lift at the corner, and naturally her stomach got all hot and stroppy. Nothing compared to how the rest of her body was reacting.

'It's nothing new. When I was twelve I was sent to a private school where many of the wealthy send their kids. I didn't fit in. Dad hadn't quite made the big league then but he wanted me to have the best. I was smart, but not filthy rich. Some of the girls were horrid to me.' Understatement. 'So I stopped going to school, hid out at the mall or the library.'

'Tell me more.'

She'd not be mentioning that they called her 'elephant'. 'When my parents found out I demanded to be sent to a public school, and not the one down the road from the private school but the one in another suburb where the chances of running into any of those awful girls were remote.'

'You got your way.' He wasn't asking.

'I was desperate. When they backed me I became determined to prove they'd made the right choice. In some ways it was harder to get ahead in the lower decile school, in others downright easy because no one wanted to knock me down all the time.' *Because on day one I arrived with a friendly smile and a willingness to fit in by keeping others happy. Three strapping brothers at my back didn't go astray either.*

'You were bullied at that private school?' His mouth tightened even before she answered.

'All the time by a roving pack of brainless bitches.' She was surprised by the strength of emotion overwhelming her as she remembered being taunted constantly, punished for things that happened, even when she hadn't been there. 'But I've moved on, grown a backbone, and become the person I want to be.' Would he believe that little white lie? Because it was a work in progress. She'd thought she'd got past those girls until Steve had undermined her confidence, resurrected her flaws. Now she knew from the bottom of her battered heart there'd be no leaping into commitment until she trusted herself to be true to Kelli, no matter what any man threw at her.

'I imagine you always had a backbone.'

'You do? Thanks.' File that one with the good stuff that came her way. Not that it was strictly correct.

The waitress arrived with their meals and cutlery, banging the plates down and shifting water glasses too hard so the contents slopped on the table.

When she'd wiped up and gone Mac asked, 'So who's the man you're avoiding by taking me to the wedding?'

'Jason Alexander. A lawyer. A friend of my brothers' from years back.'

'What's wrong with him?'

'Nothing really. He's friendly, kind, hard-working, caring. Fits in with my lot all too easily.'

Mac's eyes narrowed. 'What aren't you telling me?'

'He's too nice.'

'In other words, boring?'

'He doesn't tickle my keys.' Eek. Just the thought of Jason tickling any part of her turned her cold. 'My mother thinks he'd be *right* for me—you know, as in settle-down-with-him right.' She shuddered. 'I'm being unfair. He really is a great guy, but he doesn't do it for me.'

'How come your parents don't accept that?'

Because her ex had been cruel, selfish, and devastating in a nasty way. And because she'd been blind to his faults until he'd cut her down so painfully. 'Sometimes they're overprotective. I'm twenty-eight, but being the daughter after three sons comes with complications.'

'Am I going to be seen as the intruder?' There. A wee smile.

Might be wee, but it was powerful, switching on all her hot spots. 'Absolutely. You'll be quizzed on your intentions, asked about your favourite sport and car, and my brothers will challenge you to anything they can find, tiddlywinks if that's all there is.' Suddenly this was fun. As if Mac and she were good together. *Steady.* Getting ahead of herself. 'You're still on?'

'It's not only your brothers who put out a challenge,' he grumped. But there was laughter in his eyes. Warm and generous laughter. Rare indeed.

She melted some more. 'Where do you think I learned it from?'

The eggs were delicious, the bacon crisp and yummy. They ate in silence, Mac chewing thoughtfully. What was going on in that sharp mind? He hadn't missed a point about her family and herself, had caught on about the bullying quickly.

'Once the weekend's over and everyone's back to normal, won't the attempts to get you to date Jason resume? I won't be there to deflect them.'

'Probably, but I'll manage. I don't live at home, so it'll only be at family dinners that I'll have to confront Jason. Whereas a whole weekend is too much. I'd probably lose my rag and say something I'd regret. Jason had a bad home life and somehow became a part of our lot,' she added.

'You said you've often told Jason how you feel.'

'Yes. He just shrugs off my refusal.'

Mac went back to being quiet, finishing his meal and ordering an ice cream.

She declined one, thinking of her hips and that skintight sheath she'd be wearing at the wedding. That reminded her. 'We need to set some ground rules for the weekend.'

'Wondered when we'd have this conversation.'

'We can't have a rerun of Sydney.' *No kisses that make me boneless. Unless we follow through and don't stop at the door.*

'Which part? The ceremony? The dinner?' His smile widened, was wicked.

'Never knew you did cheeky.' He was leaving it all up to her, not making it easy. 'We have to act like a couple without getting too close, if you know what I mean.'

'I know exactly what you mean. No kissing, making out in that double bed, gazing into each other's eyes.'

'Mac!' He'd listed everything she wanted to do with him. 'Try to avoid deep and meaningful conversations with my family.'

'We've got to look believable. I'm a doctor, not an actor.' Still smiling.

She gave him one back. 'Me either. My family know me too well.'

'We'll be fine. I can be my normal aloof self and let

your family think I'm a stuck up prude who wants only to be seen and not heard.'

Laughter spluttered across her lips and she raised her hands in surrender. 'Whatever.' The weekend was looking better and better.

When Mac paid for their meals Kelli got cross. 'I pay my own way.'

'I'm your partner in crime. I don't let any woman I'm out with pay her own way.'

'We're not partners tonight,' she snapped.

'Get over yourself, because next I'm driving you home. If you're not happy about that then think of it like this. I'm getting into the role for the weekend.' No smile now.

'What? A bossy role?' She half meant it.

'That'll give you reason to dump me afterwards.'

Apart from the one about them not being compatible. *We were very compatible in Sydney.* But a string of hot kisses was not grounds for a relationship.

'Ready to go?' That exasperating smile just got more exasperating.

Kelli wanted to argue, insist she get a taxi to keep some space between them outside work until Friday, but that smile bowled over all her resolve, what little there was, and she gave up. It would be nice to be run around after by a hunk just once.

Her car was in the garage after refusing to turn over, having been untouched for six weeks. It hadn't been a flat battery so she'd had to wait until that morning to get a mechanic to come take a look. Some electrical fault that needed lots of work, and money, but she'd been offered a cut on the price if she waited until tomorrow. Seemed they were very busy, and since catching a bus to work was no big deal she'd agreed. Probably been sucked in big time, but cars were an enigma when their engines didn't turn over instantly. She'd make sure it was ready to pick up on her way to work tomorrow. Couldn't have Mac thinking he had the upper hand in case he hadn't been joking about being bossy.

After giving Mac her address Kelli sat waiting for more questions, but none came. He was too quiet. So quiet she thought she could hear his mind clicking over. Tick, tick, tick.

As her street appeared ahead she couldn't take it any more. 'What are you thinking? And don't say nothing, because I won't believe you.'

He turned the corner, parked with precision outside the house she shared with two other nurses and hauled the handbrake on before switching off the ignition.

Now the silence was deafening and Kelli's teeth were grinding while her hands were tight balls on her thighs. Somehow she managed not to yell at this infuriating man.

Shuffling that butt around on his seat, he leaned into the corner and eyeballed her. 'I want you to hear me out before shouting me down, okay?'

Her heart stuttered. 'I'll do my best.' Was this where he explained that he'd had time to think about the weekend and all the ramifications and he wanted to renege on agreeing to partner her? From what she'd observed at work Mac didn't do rushed decisions, but he had this time, so it wouldn't be a total surprise if he pulled out. There wasn't much for him in going to a stranger's wedding.

'Just checking first. How much do you want Jason What's His Name out of the picture?' Steely eyes were watching her so closely they wouldn't miss if her toes curled in her shoes.

Didn't Mac believe anything she'd said? 'Totally.' She held up her hand before he could go on. 'He's so involved with my family, whatever I do tell him is tempered with trying to be kind, yet firm.' Because her parents backed his attempts to woo her. Without their support he'd probably have found someone else by now. 'Almost like an ingrained habit.'

Mac was still watching her with that disturbing intensity.

'What?' she demanded.

He pulled further back into the corner, as though putting space between them before lobbing a bomb. 'If we pretended to be engaged, would that solve the problem?'

'Pardon?' Her ears were ringing, her head filled with strange jolts of words that weren't forming into sentences. 'Did you just say engaged? You and me?'

'I did.'

'To keep Jason out of the picture?' She wasn't buying it.

'That's the plan.'

'You don't think us sharing a room will give him pause for thought?'

'I don't know,' Mac said in that reasoned tone that irked. 'Do you?'

'Until we're back in the city and carrying on as per normal, maybe.' And, 'An engagement for the weekend isn't going to change that.'

'We could continue it for a week or two. Then when we—' he flicked his forefingers in the air '—*break up* you'll need time to get over it before you can talk to him.'

She probably would and all. 'It's a lie. I can't do that to my family.' They only wanted the best for her. That they thought Jason was the best was unfair, but not a crime. Mum was the worst offender, but the brothers didn't hold back from teasing her for letting her past get in the way of giving a good bloke a chance. Yeah, an engagement did have one or two merits. Lots of them if she thought of that blah kiss Jason had once given her, and his weak hands holding hers as he'd invited her to go to the cricket with him. She'd rather watch paint dry than watch cricket, even with a man she fancied. Mac.

No, I don't.

'Do you watch cricket?'

'There's a random question. Yes, as a matter of fact, I do. One-day games in particular.'

Still preferred the paint option. But while watching it dry she could fantasise about Mac. 'Going to a game with you wouldn't be a condition of being engaged, would it?' She watched him back as closely as he was her. Yes. There. Those lips didn't do serious nearly as often as she'd thought.

'Could be. Are you considering my suggestion?'

Suggestion? Well, it wasn't a proposal, was it? Not when there was no love involved, or just about anything else. Only a means to an end. 'We could say we haven't set a wedding date—that's the truth—and aren't in a hurry. Another truth.' Another lie. If she and Mac were engaged she'd be racing him to the altar.

'Sure. If we have to say anything at all. Won't your family be too tied up with the current wedding to be thinking ahead to another?'

'Mac, you have no idea what you've let yourself in for.' She shook her head at him. 'Mum will start planning the moment I mention an engagement.'

'Maybe we shouldn't, then. Just look so lovey-dovey that they'll be nudging each other and asking when we might be wanting to tie the knot.'

'Do you have to look ill when you say that?' For some inexplicable reason that stung, badly. Was she so unattractive he couldn't imagine being lovey-dovey around her again?

Suddenly her hands were being lifted from her thighs

and strong fingers wrapped around her fists. 'You're so lovely I want…' Mac gasped, swallowed. 'It's the reality of what we're doing hitting home. I'm not changing my mind. But it isn't going to be as easy as I'd first thought. My suggestion just made it harder.'

'It was never going to be straightforward, but then I know my family. They want so much for me to be happy, they don't see that I can be that without settling down.' She'd thought she'd found Mr Right once, truly believed he loved her for who she was, what she was, hadn't seen the disdain coming when she ate a cake or took a day off from the gym. Apparently she needed to watch her figure with the intensity a native falcon would prowl the vineyards for birds. And he'd expected her to be glamorous when they socialised with his colleagues.

'You don't ever want to get married?' Mac's fingers tightened, loosened again.

'It would take some convincing from a very determined man.' She gazed into the eyes of the man she was learning didn't give up easily. She might be ready to get a life but Mac seemed to have issues he wasn't letting go in a hurry.

Doubts pushed forward. 'Mac.' She sucked in a breath. 'I need to know more about why you're doing this for me.'

He sighed. 'I've kind of been waiting for that.'

Well? Was he going to tell her? Because if not then she had to think seriously about her stance. Patience wasn't her strong point, but somehow she found some and waited quietly, her gut churning.

'Someone once helped me when I was in a bad place and I've never forgotten it.'

'You're saying I'm in a bad place?'

'Not bad, but you need help to extricate yourself from

a tricky situation, and I want to be the guy to see you through it.'

Her heart was turning mushy. 'What can I say?'

He smiled. 'Thanks would work.'

She started leaning forward with the intention of kissing him thank you, and stopped. Kisses were incendiary between them and now was not the time for an inferno. 'Thanks.' But she still wasn't satisfied he'd told her everything behind his generous offer.

'Hopefully I can give you time to sort yourself out, get rid of that despair that sneaks into your eyes when you think no one's looking.'

'What?' She stared at him. He was too astute for her good.

'Something's worrying you and I don't think it's all about Jason.' He held up a hand. 'It's all right. I'm not asking you to talk about things you'd rather not, just letting you know I'm here for you any time you want to unload.'

Run, Kelli, run. Now, while you can. Before your heart decides he's the one for you.

She didn't know how to answer, couldn't tell him her hang-ups, her need to find her own way before joining up with someone for life.

The silence grew between them, not uncomfortable, but not endearing either. Finally Mac gave her a lopsided smile. 'So are we engaged or not?'

No. He read her too easily. Forewarned was forearmed, wasn't it? There was something warm and comforting about being with a man who understood her. She could enjoy the fantasy and relax over the weekend knowing she was safe from the digs about Jason. Tempting. Too tempting. 'Yes,' she answered before she allowed all those pesky doubts and honesty factors to change her mind.

Mac straightened up, giving a tight little laugh as he

reached to pull on his seat belt. 'That's that, then. I've just got engaged and I don't know what to say.'

'Hardly how I imagined it to go either.' Nothing like when Steve proposed. Roses, champagne, a rock on a ring. Clichés in hindsight. Kelli elbowed the door open. 'But thank you for offering to be my partner, engaged or otherwise. I'm starting to look forward to the weekend. I adore my brothers and this is a special occasion.' She sighed at the imagined sight of the guys all dressed up in their tuxes and Billy's eyes filled with love for his lady, his second chance at happiness. 'I promise to make sure you have a great time.'

'As long as they don't want to draw pistols at dawn I'm sure I can get through without too much stress.' This time the smile was soft and genuine, and for her.

Too many of those and she would be in trouble. Mac's smiles, gentle and warm, were hidden treasure. They wound around her, bolstered her courage to do the things she wanted for herself. Including going to the wedding with him. Come next Monday she'd probably be regretting this, but, hey, she could make the most of what Mac was giving her.

'The guys aren't monsters, just overprotective of me.' They'd been the ones to take retribution on the bullies at the private school. They'd also dropped by the new school to show solidarity if anyone was thinking she might be a pushover—which she was. But instead of their getting people's backs up the girls in her class had become firm friends so that they'd get invited home and could spend time hanging with her brothers.

'Glad to hear it,' Mac growled. 'One more thing. I don't have your phone number. Nor you mine. Fiancés probably should be able to get in touch with each other.'

'Fair enough.' She rattled off her number then waited

for Mac to text so she had his. 'Done.' Slipping out of the vehicle, she smothered a yawn. It had been a huge day. 'See you at work.' A great way for a newly engaged woman to say goodnight to her fiancé.

'Goodnight, Kelli.'

The engine started but Mac didn't pull away until she'd let herself in the front door of the house. Admirable, but a hot kiss would've gone a lot further.

'Bleeding heck, what have I done?' she whispered, her shoulder hard against the doorframe as she watched the tail-lights of Mac's four-wheel drive disappear around the corner. Jumped in the deep end of a monster pool with weights on her feet, that was what.

Mac concentrated on driving, nothing else. He couldn't let anything into his mind or he'd lose focus and go through a red light or cross the middle line or something equally dangerous.

Dangerous? That was exactly where he was at with Kelli. With her warmth, and sense of fun, and stunning looks, and, damn it, everything about her, she threatened all his barriers, undermined his need to stay self-contained, uninvolved, out of another relationship. He'd had the ultimate love with Cherie. A man didn't get that twice. And if by some twisted stroke of fate he did, he'd be on tenterhooks for the rest of his life waiting for the axe to fall again.

Focus, driving only, remember?

He'd smiled when Kelli had explained her brothers were protective of her. Because it was great there were people to guard her back. Not because he couldn't help himself and had to let those warm feelings out. Not that.

Relief rocked him. Kelli wasn't interested in this guy Jason. She hadn't run for the hills when *he'd* offered to be her partner. Was she keen on him? A little bit? Well, she'd stayed in the car when he'd suggested the engagement thing. Went to show she wasn't thinking straight because it really had been one of the wackiest ideas he'd ever come up with.

Toot, toot. A car sped past, the occupants waving fists at him.

He glanced around. So much for concentrating on driving. The four-wheel drive was stopped in the middle of an intersection, the indicator flashing for left when he needed to go right. Thankfully it was well beyond midnight and the traffic was light to non-existent now that those unhappy fist-wavers had gone past.

Do I tickle your keys, Kelli?

She hadn't been shy in coming forward that night in Sydney, had kissed him as fiercely as he'd kissed her. It had been a one-off night, brought on by too much champagne and watching their friends all gooey-eyed for each other. Had to have been, or his world was slowly tipping off its axis.

They were about to spend a weekend together at another wedding celebration, under the microscopic watch of people who cared for Kelli. Could they pull it off, or would it soon become obvious he was a fraud? All he asked was that if the family learned the truth they went easy on him because technically he was on their side.

That need to protect was alive and kicking, with Kelli in its sights, whatever the cost to himself.

CHAPTER FOUR

'LET'S GET YOU to X-ray,' Kelli told the middle-aged woman sitting awkwardly on the bed, grimacing with pain whenever she moved. 'You do need to breathe occasionally, you know,' she added gently.

'How can I, when it makes my ribs shift?' Holly muttered.

'Bit tricky, eh?'

'Stupid ram. What was his problem anyway?'

'You didn't see him coming?' Kelli waited for Holly to ease herself upright.

'Never had cause to worry with this ram before. Every now and then we get a bolshie one and know to stay well clear until we find a place for him on a farm somewhere, but Angus has always been so docile.'

'You should've brought him in here for a check-up too. Could be something's got him in a twist.' Kelli chuckled.

'My husband's taking him to the vet once he's got me back home. At least he put me first,' she joked. 'What happens if my ribs are broken?'

Kelli sucked air through her teeth. 'You're not going to like this but plenty of rest so as not to jar those ribs.'

'That's not happening.' They headed along the corridor to the elevator bank. 'Painkillers?'

'Absolutely.' Kelli punched the button for the second

floor. 'Do you have another job apart from looking after the sheep at Cornwall Park?'

'We spend a lot of time helping on our son's farm in Karaka. His wife is disabled and requires a lot of care. I'm more patient with the stock so I'm kept outside.'

'Families, eh?' Kelli had yet to break the news to her parents that she was 'engaged', and was wondering if it would be best to keep that gem on hold, only to be used in extreme circumstances. They now knew she was bringing Mac, but nothing more. Reluctance at fibbing railed against the need to be able to enjoy Billy's wedding.

There was a lot more to Mac than she knew about. Like what had caused him to fall into that dark place he'd mentioned? She was starting to see past that barrier he kept in place, especially at work. He'd obviously been hurt and naturally wanted to protect himself from it happening again. Had a woman he loved dumped him? Or did his pain go back further, to childhood or his teen years? He wasn't one for putting anything about himself out there, so to have told her as much as he had said that he trusted her. Which meant she couldn't press for more info, had to wait until he was ready to share. Another sigh. She'd take this one day at a time.

After the elevator whisked her patient away Kelli returned to the counter to see who was next. It was pointless spending time thinking about what made Mac tick. The answers weren't here, at work, or if they were she wasn't seeing anything other than his medical skills and caring nature. If she was going to learn more about her *fiancé* she'd have to ask him some pointed questions. Not that he'd likely answer them.

'Take a break,' Stephanie told her before she reached the counter.

'I'll be in the cafeteria, too,' Mac informed the head

nurse, who immediately locked her gaze on Kelli and gave an almost imperceptible nod.

Almost. Not quite. 'What was that about?' Mac asked.

'Ask Stephanie,' Kelli retorted and dived into her bag for the salad she'd put in there earlier.

'Best not.' Mac opened a bag of crisps as they walked out of the department and offered them to her.

'No, thanks.' That dress was so form-fitting one chip might make all the difference to how she looked on the day.

'Talked to your family today?'

Her cell phone had been remarkably quiet most of the day. Possibly too quiet. It wouldn't mean her mother had dropped the date issue even knowing it was solved. She'd want all the details on Mac. 'I phoned to tell them they could relax because I was bringing a wonderful man to the wedding who I couldn't wait for them to meet.'

'Wonderful, eh?'

Naturally he'd pick up on that. He was a man. 'Don't get carried away. I could hardly say you were an uptight, pompous type.'

'I'm surprised you didn't.' He actually laughed and held out a chair for her at a table in the cafeteria. 'Any mention of the other?'

As in engagement? 'I thought it could wait until the last minute. I already turned down an invitation to dinner tonight.' Thank goodness for night shifts.

'Do you want to wear a ring?' Mac was studying his crisps too intently. They were only potato chips.

'Are you serious? That would be going too far.' She was almost shouting, and at the shock on Mac's face she pulled on the brakes. 'I figured on saying we haven't had time to choose one yet.'

'That's fairly close to the truth, I guess.' Now he

seemed to be interested in watching her again. Which was more exciting? Her or the crisps? 'You'd better give me the lowdown on what I'm expected to wear to the wedding.'

'Do you own an evening suit?'

His eyes crinkled at the edges. 'Yes, mam. And a morning one, some business ones, and others.'

'You're a suit man.' There was something about a good-looking man dressed in a suit and tie that made her all gooey inside. Mac had looked awesome in the stylish one he'd worn as Conor's best man in Sydney. She blamed that suit for losing her composure with him. Along with the dancing, the atmosphere, her friend's happiness after a difficult few years. But the suit had been the start of her emotions and hormones spiralling out of control. Navy with a crisp white shirt and emerald-green tie to match her dress. Oh, yes.

'You're looking decidedly dreamy,' Mac noted. 'Care to share?'

No way this side of Christmas. Or any time after. Knowing he'd made her feel happy and safe and even okay-looking that night would be giving Mac ammunition to tell her the opposite. As Steve had done, time and time again. She shuddered. Mac wouldn't do that. He was too kind. Or was she once again being naïve? 'More likely that's tiredness. I was late to bed last night, and up early.'

Bed. Another loaded word. They were going to be sharing one for two whole nights. After another wedding, where Mac would wear a suit, and she would get all excited. 'You going to take your PJs?'

A bark of laughter cut across her musings. 'The last time I wore those I was ten.'

'They wouldn't fit.' A giggle was starting. The idea of Mac in pyjamas was so not turning her on. Exactly the point she'd been trying to make, but the image in her head of him was hilarious and the giggles won out. 'I can sort of picture you in striped pants and top.'

'Racing cars.'

'Truly?'

'Yep.' He grinned, a rare sight that zapped her in the tummy and woke up those butterflies behind her ribs. When Mac relaxed the grip on his emotions he was a sight dreams were made of. His handsome face became beyond wonderful, good-looking mixed with fun and care and enjoyment. And sex. His green eyes reminded her of spring fields, and that mouth... That mouth could be soft as cotton wool, as demanding as a hungry child, as heat provoking as a firelighter.

She wasn't going to survive the weekend. Not and come out sane at the other end. She was going to be in a constant state of terror in case she jumped his bones or fell under his spell and had, not one, but two sensual nights in bed.

Rules, Kells. You've got rules in place.

Rules were made to be broken.

Her phone vibrated. Tugging it free of her pocket, she answered, 'Hi, Mum.' For once her mother's timing was perfect. 'Did you get the florist sorted?' Her mother was chef de mission for the wedding since Billy's fiancée, Leanne, didn't have family in New Zealand to support her apart from some cousins who were keener on partying than preparing for the big day.

'Of course I did. Now, my girl, we're dying to meet Mac. What about lunch tomorrow before you both start work? Just your dad and I.'

Shouldn't have answered the phone. Once again out of the pan and into the heat. 'Not tomorrow, Mum. I've got to pick up my car, and get my dress from the dry-cleaner's.'

She'd finished the hem on Sunday and taken the dress in for a professional finish yesterday.

'You making excuses, by any chance, Kelli Barnett?'

Yes, Mum, and I've got more up my sleeve if I need them.

'This week is about Billy and Leanne, not Mac and I.'

Across the table Mac looked up from the crossword he'd begun filling in. His nod was in agreement.

'We were thinking if Mac met us before the weekend it would be easier for him on Friday night when he's amongst the whole tribe.'

Why did that have to sound so darned reasonable? 'Believe me, Mac won't have any problem fitting in.'

'Why are you hedging, my girl?'

Because she loved her mother to bits she gave in. 'Mac, have you got a spare hour tomorrow to have lunch with my parents?' *Say no, you're getting your hair done, or meeting with the Prime Minister about a dog, or you don't do lunch.*

'No problem. What time and where?'

Thanks a bundle. He looked so at ease she wanted to biff him upside of his head. The uptight version did have a place—like right about now. But what could she do? 'You hear that, Mum?'

'Twelve-thirty at Cardo's.' She'd heard all right. No doubt her ear was pressed so hard against the phone it hurt. 'Looking forward to meeting this man who's caught your interest.'

Kelli shuddered as she slipped her phone back into her pocket. 'Game on.'

'I can pull out if that'd make you happier,' Mac said in such a reasonable voice that she wanted to curl up and cry.

'What have I done? It's not as if Mum and Dad are bad people, yet I'm lying to them.'

'Remember why we're doing this.'

He'd said we. As in they were together in this pickle. 'Because I've run out of ways to deflect him without being a complete cow, and I can't do that.'

'So I'm the deflection.' Mac shook his head and smiled. 'Pleased to meet you. I'm Mr Deflection.'

'Stop it, you're making me feel better.'

'That's the whole idea, Kelli.' He glanced down at the crossword, filled in a word, then began tapping the pen on the page. 'Was there another man who caused you strife in the past for your family to be wanting to pair you off with the apparently very pleasant Jason?'

'Do you need to know this to be my fiancé?'

Mac locked his eyes on her. 'I think I do.'

That'd mean exposing her flaws—before the weekend.

Mac added, 'I'd like to know more about you.'

He sounded so genuine the words just spilled. 'Two years ago I was engaged to an up-and-coming plastic surgeon.' An ego with lots of ideas on how to improve her body and looks. 'No one in the family liked him. He was cold and calculating, but I was smitten and wouldn't hear a bad word about him.' Until the day he demanded she have breast reduction surgery and a butt tuck. He explained that if she refused he wouldn't take her to any of the swanky parties he liked to attend. An irrational fear of going under the knife had won out over her uncertainties about her appearance. By a very narrow margin. End of engagement.

'What changed your mind?' Mac asked softly, the crossword now lying on the table, forgotten.

'One day he was so insulting about my appearance and other attributes I had to take a long, hard look at him. Didn't like what I saw.' He'd made her feel worthless. 'I'd made a mistake and for a while doubted my ability to judge people.' That sounded easier than it had been. Still, some things were best kept under wraps, and lots of clever clothes.

'So your family want to protect you from that happening again?'

She nodded. 'When I broke it off with him, Steve was furious, humiliated me every which way he could. That upset my parents more than anything and is probably why I'm in this spot.'

'Well, we're going to prove you're up to making the right choices,' Mac concluded.

Knowing Mac was prepared to go in to bat for her was as if a huge weight had been lifted. 'You're saying you're right for me?' she asked cheekily. 'That no one can fault you as my partner?'

'Your words, not mine,' he laughed, then sobered. 'If you want to change your mind I won't stop you. It's your call.'

Not so together, then. At the same time Mac wasn't telling her what to do, which earned him points. 'We're still on. For the first time in months I'm excited about the wedding.' And not all that excitement was down to her brother's big day. Some of it came from the company she'd be keeping, however temporary.

Stephanie appeared beside them. 'Incoming chest pains, tachycardia. I've got no one else available.'

'Coming.' Mac stood and began heading for the department.

'You're not taking your mug up to the counter?' Kelli called all innocently.

'Thought you'd do it for me,' he shot over his shoulder. 'As forward payment.'

'I think I liked you better when you were serious and

proper.' But she smiled as she picked up his mug along with hers. Mac did that to her.

A little after eleven that night Kelli hit the gym. Running another seven Ks would counter the effects of last night's bacon and eggs. She shouldn't have had them, but she'd been hungry and had wanted comfort food to minimise the anxiety beginning to build up over Mac's role in the coming weekend.

All the treadmills were in use except for one. Right beside the one Mac was using. Kelli resisted the urge to curse. Hadn't he gone up to the surgical ward to talk to a patient they'd sent to Theatre earlier that night?

The treadmill was out. She needed space while she mulled over the dross banging around in her head. The rowing machines were right in his line of vision, a sight she understood too well after watching him last night. Mac was not getting an eyeful of her pulling on that equipment, sweating and puffing like him the night before.

The cycle machine was it. Her least favourite. The way those bike seats embedded themselves in her backside was horrid and always seemed to leave her feeling like tenderised meat. But sore backside, or ogled butt? She'd take the pain any day.

'The humidity isn't helping,' Mac gasped as she passed him.

'Eighty per cent last I heard.'

'You're not running tonight?' he asked when she didn't climb onto the adjacent treadmill.

'Thought I'd go for the cycles instead. Nothing like a good ride.'

Mac's eyes widened and he looked at her as he had that night in Sydney. As if he wanted her. Heat radiated off him. Flipping her head sideways, she tried to avoid his need, sure she was giving back an identical message. Her nipples were peaks pushing against her tee shirt, her sex hot and damp.

'Cycling it is,' Mac retorted, bringing her instantly out of her delirium.

Thank goodness. Something had to. She was standing in the gym, not outside a hotel bedroom. Right, on with the job. Anything to shut down her mind, put Mac on hold. Ah, put Mac aside for ever.

Earplugs in and the music loud. Deliberately setting a higher than her normal speed, Kelli shuffled her butt left and right on the seat to get as comfortable as possible and began to cycle, building up the speed slowly. It wasn't long before sweat ran down her spine, between her aching, thwarted breasts, and had her top clinging to her skin wherever it touched. Yuk.

Mac stopped running, headed over to the weights, and the air did not feel any lighter.

Puff, puff. This cycling was hard yakker tonight, for some reason. Glancing around to see if anyone was watching she pressed the button to lower the resistance by two notches. No point in killing herself before the weekend.

Sometimes she wished she had the strength to ignore the fact she was on the larger side and didn't have to put her body through all this trauma. Imagine not having to work herself into a sweat ball five days a week. But any time she even half-heartedly contemplated not going to the gym she'd think of Steve and his scalpel. Giving herself the weekends off was her treat, and definitely her favourite days of the week.

Thirty minutes later Mac tapped the back of her hand and waited until she'd cleared her ears of music. 'You going to be all night on that thing?'

'Nothing better to do.' Her thighs were aching and her glutes were so tenderised they were ready for the barbecue.

'You need a life, girl. How about another round at the All-Nighter?'

Then she'd have to row, cycle *and* run tomorrow. 'Best offer I've had all week. No, make that since you offered to be my partner.' Her legs were slowing. 'Are you finished here?'

He nodded and slashed at his moist cheeks. 'Can't get enthused.'

'Enthused? Over exercise? Are you nuts?'

Mac's eyes narrowed. 'If you feel like that why come here? It's not as though you're overweight or in need of a body makeover.'

Was the guy blind? Thoughtlessly she leaned in, brushed her lips against his, hesitated and began a full-on kiss. 'Thank you,' she murmured against him.

Firm hands were on her shoulders, gently pushing her back, away from that divine man with his lovely compliments. 'Much as I hate to stop you, we are in the middle of the hospital gym where colleagues are working out—with their eyes wide open.'

Oh. Right. Of course. 'Sorry.' *He doesn't want to be seen with me.*

'Kelli, stop saying sorry. You didn't do anything wrong. I'm thinking more that you won't like the gossip mill starting up about us.'

Mac was protecting her from the gossips?

Go, you, Mac Taylor. I could really get used to this.

No, she couldn't, shouldn't, wouldn't. Her family already tried to protect her and look how she objected when they stole some of her independence. 'Shower time.'

His mouth lifted. 'I suppose.'

'See you in ten.'

'Twice as long as last night?'

She was sweatier than last night. *And* she needed to give Mac time to forget asking why she might say sorry so often. If she even did.

She did.

Sorry appeased people, kept them from giving her a hard time. Sorry didn't always work. It most definitely was a habit she needed to break.

Starting now. Tonight. No more 'sorry' unless there was a very strong reason, and that didn't include trying to keep people onside.

Hey, didn't Mac say he'd hated stopping her kiss? Forget sorry, think about what that might mean. He wanted more kisses from her. Yes. Mentally punching the air, she headed for the showers.

Mac watched Kelli fork up her salad. 'Who eats lettuce at twelve-thirty in the morning?'

'Me.' Chew, chew. Add in a slice of tomato.

'You don't look half as happy as you did last night eating bacon and eggs.'

She swallowed and glared first at him and then at her plate. 'You're right. But last night was an indulgence. Tonight is reality.'

'There's not enough lettuce on your plate to keep a rabbit happy.' Was she a diet freak? 'You have a figure that'd send any man into raptures.'

'I like to keep on top of my weight.' Kelli looked everywhere but at him.

'Do me a favour and have something tasty and filling to go with that salad. I'd hate you to fade away to a stick insect.'

She blanched. 'Fat chance.'

'Kelli, girl, you're not fat. You're perfect. Tall and shapely, not thin and scrawny.'

She looked at him as though he'd lost his mind. 'Shapely is another word for plump.'

Reaching for Kelli's free hand, he wrapped it in his fingers, felt her tremble. 'Whoever told you that is an ass. Or worse. Personally, I don't want to feel bones when I hug a woman. I want her warmth and curves and softness.' Not that he'd done much hugging for a long time. He used to love hugs. There was something relaxed and friendly and caring between two people who were close when they hugged. Like saying the world was good.

'Each to their own.' Hope tripped through her gaze.

'Well, you're my partner so I get to say what I like.' When they called it all off he would still think Kelli had a body to die for. He should ask his mother to start sending her care packages. As if that'd go down well with this prickly woman. 'Feel like ice cream tonight?' he teased, aware she'd hate him asking, but wanting to show her there was no harm in indulging occasionally. As long as she was healthy and stayed that way, eating was all about balance.

'I hate you,' she muttered as she stared longingly at the menu listing a multitude of ice-cream flavours.

'I know.' Did she realise he was still holding her hand? He should withdraw but this was cool. Cosy. Nice. Something he hadn't done since… Cherie. Mac sat back, taking his hand away. From another chance at happiness.

Happiness was good; everyone deserved it. Even he did. Maybe. But when happiness went belly up then… Then the pain was unbearable. Terrifying. Inexplicable. It tore a man apart, left him unable to put the pieces back together, definitely not the way they'd been before.

Cherie's death had changed him. The loss of their child

before he or she had seen the light of day had crippled him. But losing Cherie had been indescribable. All he really knew was he couldn't face that again. The guilt at not realising what was happening still ate at him, demanded a price be paid. Staying single and focused on helping as many folk as possible through his career was that price, and one he was comfortable with.

So Kelli. He was more than okay with helping her out as long as he kept his mind-set in front. Mac swallowed the bile at the back of his throat. Irony was a bitter pill. He'd offered to be Kelli's fiancé for the weekend. For longer if that was what it took to sort out Jason. But he couldn't take on the role for real. As tempting as it might become. He would not. That meant opening his heart wide, letting Kelli in to everything that made him tick, risking hurt.

Kelli was pushing away from the table. 'Time I headed home. See you tomorrow.'

'Not so fast.' Mac was upright, the tab in his hand. 'I'll get this then give you a ride home.'

Ride. That damned word again. When Kelli had used it earlier his brain had not been picturing her sitting in his four-wheel drive, that was for sure.

Nor had hers if that cute shade of pink pouring into her cheeks was an indicator.

'I don't need you running around after me.'

'So you said last night, and I'm giving back the same reply. I am giving you a—lift.' Better, not perfect, but one degree up from ride. 'I heard you tell your mother your car is in the workshop until tomorrow.' Sensible talk might abate the growing need to touch this tantalising woman, to hold her close and feel her skin against his, and kiss her until his world spun. Might. Didn't. His world was already spinning. He wanted a hug and kiss. He wanted the whole nine yards. With Kelli. The sex nine yards, not the commitment nine yards. Which made him a heel. Not who he was or wanted to be.

'Tomorrow I'll pick you up for lunch as repayment,' Miss Independence muttered.

Tomorrow was another day. Tomorrow his head and body would be back under control and he'd be able to talk sense. Tonight he was all out of any kind of sense. 'Let's go.'

The sooner they hit the road, the sooner he'd be on his own and able to loosen off the tension gripping him in unexpected places. This *was* only a fleeting problem.

CHAPTER FIVE

'Hi, Mum,' Kelli answered her phone. 'How's your day going?'

'From bad to worse. I can't make lunch, my girl. Those imbeciles at the catering company say they can't get crayfish for the entrée. Something about an order not going through. I can forgive them that, everyone makes mistakes.'

Huh? Can I have whatever it is you're on, Mum? 'But?'

'They've done nothing about coming up with a suitable replacement dish. The wedding's only three days away. What's wrong with these people?' Her distress poured through the ether.

'Take a breath, Mum. A big one.' *Think, Kelli, think. Find a solution. Mum needs a solution.* 'Do you know where the caterers were getting the crayfish from?'

'The caterers said the Kaikoura region but supplies are intermittent from there since the earthquake so you'd think they'd have outsourced further afield.'

'You could have a chicken entrée. A vegetarian one.'

'Wash your mouth out, my girl. This is me you're suggesting that to. The queen of organising events does not take a soft option when something goes wrong.'

How true. Mum hated to be wrong-footed.

So think of something. Someone. Ah.

'Jack Harris. You know, Andy's mate from university. He runs a fishing company in Milford Sound. Lots of crayfish down there. Get Andy to call him asap.'

'Kelli, darling, you're a gem. Why didn't I think of that? Jack's coming up for the wedding, too.'

Kelli let out a relieved sigh. 'He can bring cartons of live lobsters under his arm.'

'Have you got an answer for my next problem?' Mum asked. 'I've learned this morning that one of the bridesmaids gets seasick *and* airsick.'

'The helicopter will be a lot faster than the ferry. Fill her up with travel pills but don't overdose her as she'll need to be fully compos once she's on Waiheke.'

'My thoughts exactly. Guess there's really no other way round this one. I'll go talk to my friendly pharmacist.'

'You've got a busy morning, Mum.'

'I'm sorry to cancel lunch. I've got too much to sort out. And your father's busy with his Sydney counterpart.' Not a lot of conviction in Mum's voice about Dad being unable to do lunch. That was definitely an add-on. 'Friday will have to be it.'

'Sure, not a problem.' The relief at her reprieve just wasn't coming. Instead disappointment was the dominating emotion. She wanted her parents to meet Mac? Today instead of Friday? *Not making sense here, Kelli.*

Mac was a temporary fix, not a lifelong commitment. Commitment? Didn't she mean decision? Commitment? No way. He was a sexy hunk, an intelligent man with a sense of humour that he occasionally let out of the bag, but commitment material? When she wasn't ready to commit to anyone? Hadn't completely laid the past to bed? Mac never hesitated saying she looked good, which gave her hope and relief and some happiness. But… But she wasn't one hundred per cent certain she could trust herself in believing him. She'd once believed Steve loved her and look how that ended.

'You still there, Kelli?'

'Friday night it is.' When there would be a crowd of family to dilute the impact on Mac and hopefully not scare him away until after the wedding.

Next she called Mac. 'Lunch's cancelled. Mum's got problems to sort for Saturday.'

'Let's go anyway. I'll still pick you up a little after twelve.' Click.

Thought I was picking you up.

This was a bit like a date. No, it was a date. Possibly a backhanded one, but she and Mac going out. She needed to get a wriggle on and collect her car, then go get her dress from the dry-cleaner's. Then make sure she looked perfect for her 'date'. With Mac. A smile lifted her mouth and warmth crept in under her skin. That skirt and the blouse with three-quarter-length sleeves she'd created for autumn were about to get their first outing.

Stop it. You're getting too keen on the man, and there are no guarantees he won't hurt you.

If only she could drop the mantra. Learn to accept who she was and demand everyone else do the same.

Mac held open the four-wheel drive's door, his gaze fixed on her thighs. 'You look stunning. Is that skirt new?'

Kelli automatically ran her hand down the soft leather of her short black skirt, one she hadn't had any opportunities to wear, what with being away in Fiji since the weather had begun to cool into autumn. It fitted perfectly and the red top made to hide her large breasts wasn't too shabby either. But stunning? 'You say the nicest things.'

'Kelli,' Mac growled. 'I mean it. I am not trying to

suck up to you by uttering niceties for the sake of it. If I hadn't liked the effect I'd have kept quiet.'

That took her breath away, along with the ability to reply. Mac believed she looked stunning. Those butterflies started up behind her ribs, flappity flap. He was way more than a quick fix to her weekend problem. With an abrupt nod she concentrated on pulling her seat belt into place. Her fingers weren't as steady as they should be, and those butterflies had relatives beating in her tummy. Stunning. Might be an exaggeration, but she could live with that. Enjoy it, grab it and pretend it was true—until proven otherwise. *How's that for standing strong?*

Mac pulled out onto the street. 'Will the booking at Cardo's still be available?'

'Yes.' Cardo's always had a table available for her family or any Barnett family business meals. 'Are you sure you want to go there? I don't mind if you change the plan.'

'And miss out on the best seafood ravioli in the city? I don't think so.'

'You frequent Cardo's?' The man had taste. What was there not to like about him? Like? Try adore. Something stronger? L-lo... No. No. Please no. Her mouth clamped shut.

'I wouldn't say frequent, but I go there occasionally when I can't be bothered to make my own pasta, or I need to get out of the apartment for a few hours because I'm sick of my own company.'

The clamp slipped. 'You make your own pasta?' This man just kept on getting better and better. He wasn't only a very good doctor and a good-looking hunk at the gym. He made pasta. Please, not the L word. That would wreck everything.

'Beats the packet stuff any day.' Mac smiled. Or was that a smirk?

'Who'd have thought it? Where did you learn to do that?'

'Mum's parents came out from Italy to Wellington sixty years ago.'

'So you grew up on Italian food. I'm so jealous.'

'Don't be. We only had it as a treat. My father thought eating pasta was like eating flour and water.' The smile had gone, his mouth now grim. 'He refused any kind of Italian food.'

'You aren't close?' Definitely some problem there. His hands were gripping the steering wheel and his arms were tight. As were his thighs, she noted as she cruised down his body.

'Not at all. He passed away ten years ago.' The four-wheel drive jerked as Mac roared away on the green light. 'We didn't see eye to eye on anything.'

Thoughtlessly she placed her hand on his forearm, felt the tension in the muscles under her palm. Went to withdraw, decided against it. 'I'm sorry.'

Mac didn't shrug her away. 'Don't worry about it. It's old hat.'

Yes, and still hurts. 'I got lucky. My family might be bossy and like to run my life for me at times, but we are close. Even the two, soon to be three, sisters-in-law fit right in.'

'Is that another reason for them foisting Jason on you? He already fits in.'

'You might have a point. He's someone we all know well, no hidden agendas.'

'Interesting.'

Maybe. 'Did you grow up in Wellington?' She needed to know stuff too, right?

'Yep, Lyall Bay, where many Italians settled years back. Dad desperately wanted to move away but as my *nonno* bought the house I grew up in as a wedding gift to my parents Dad was tied. Something he resented all his married life.'

'*Nonno?* Grandfather?'

'Yeah. A fabulous old guy. Loved him to bits.' The tension backed off.

Loved, as in the past. Someone else Mac had lost. 'Your mother?'

'Still lives in the same house, only now it's party central for seniors. My word, not hers. She is getting older and wiser, but she's not a senior, if you please.' Mac was smiling softly. 'Croquet, Bridge games, Tai Chi. You name it, it happens at Maria's place.'

Kelli had never seen him so relaxed. His mother was special to him. 'Do you get to see her often?'

'I try to get down every couple of months, but I don't always make it. I'm going the weekend after the wedding.'

'You didn't cancel this weekend for me, did you?' She'd feel terrible when Mac obviously adored his mother.

'No. It's her birthday in ten days and I'm taking a crowd of her cronies to dinner at one of the top restaurants in town. Can you imagine what that's going to be like? A dozen seniors who think they're teenagers in wrinkly skin.'

The laughter wouldn't hold back. Kelli bent forward as it roared out of her. 'Bedlam, I reckon,' she finally managed to gasp. 'You are going to be toast, mister. They will give you endless teasing and stress.' What she wouldn't give to see that.

'You're sounding too gleeful. Might have to extend the engagement to cover the following weekend. Wouldn't my fiancée attend her future mother-in-law's birthday?'

Careful what you wish for, Kelli. Not laughing now.

'You'd tell her the same stuff we're going to tell my family? For what reason?'

'To make you eat your words.' He grinned back. 'But no, I won't do that. She'd get too excited and smother you with love and questions.'

'Your mother wants you settled down?' It did make sense. Mac had to be in his mid-thirties. 'How old are you?'

'Yes, she does. Thirty-six. And before you ask, I am a widower.'

Her lungs deflated like popped balloons. The fun evaporated. The black hole he'd fallen into. The reason he kept aloof—except not always with her. No idea what that meant. 'That's sad. Awful. Hell, I don't know what to say.'

'You're doing fine.' Mac flicked her a dark look. 'It's all been said a hundred times. Don't get me wrong, I'm grateful that people care enough to say something. It's just that it doesn't make a handful of difference.' He drew a breath. 'Thank you for caring.'

For a man who didn't put much out there that was some speech. 'So time's not the greatest healer?' Did this explain why he'd left her that night? Not because he'd changed his mind about her, but because he'd remembered how much he loved his wife?

He grunted. 'I guess it has helped. It's been four years. Sometimes I feel as though she went only yesterday, but more often lately I am aware it's been a long while.' He scrubbed a hand down his face. 'But not long enough.'

'This was what you were referring to when I asked why you were helping me.'

'Yeah.' His fingers were tight on the steering wheel. 'After Cherie died I was in a bad place. Not sleeping, barely eating, struggling to get through a day's work without making mistakes. Basically I hated being alive.' His chest rose, fell back. 'My mentor at the hospital turned up one morning and hauled me out of ED, drove me to his cabin two hours away in the hills where there was nothing, no one, but the trees, the weather and the birds.'

'That'd be confronting.'

'It got more so. Tom stayed the first night with me, told me how I'd nearly screwed up with a patient—I hadn't even noticed—and that I had to get my act together. He understood what I was going through because he'd lost his wife two years earlier. Then he just sat and waited and, sure enough, the words spilled, my pain, my grief, not understanding why it had to happen to me and Cherie, everything.' His voice was barely a whisper.

Kelli laid her hand on his thigh.

'He left the next morning, telling me he'd be back at the end of the week. Thought I'd go mad at first. The bush was quiet, even the birdsong didn't register with me. With nothing to occupy my mind I couldn't hold back all the images of Cherie and our future I'd been denying.' Mac cleared his throat. 'Anyway, I survived the week and went back to work totally focused on why I was there. Tom saved me that day, and I'll never forget it.'

Out of words without sounding crass or condescending, Kelli kept quiet for the rest of the ride to the restaurant. But her mind whirled. No wonder he was so serious. Or had appeared to be until she'd begun getting to know him better. How did anyone get over losing the love of their life? Because that was who Mac's wife would've been. He didn't do things by halves, would've loved her with all his being. Kelli had been devastated when her ninety-two-year-old grandmother died quietly in her sleep one night after a good innings. Nothing like what Mac must've dealt with.

'Must be my lucky day,' Mac said with forced lightness as he swung into a park directly over the road from Cardo's.

Kelli placed her hand in his forearm. Touching him a lot lately. 'If you want to cancel I won't beat you up.'

'Miss out on tortellini? I don't think so. Come on. Hustle your butt, woman. I'm starving.' This time there was warmth in his voice and a soft smile that went straight to her belly to spread heat in all directions. Which was not a good idea when she'd just learned that Mac wasn't in the running for a new partner. He was still grieving for his wife.

Definitely the wake-up call she needed to get back on track with keeping their bizarre relationship story working and not spreading into something neither of them wanted. Because, despite feeling closer to Mac than ever before, she wasn't ready for a relationship. Strange how she had to keep reminding herself when being with Mac felt so right. 'Pizza for me.'

'Eat some real food, woman. You'll work it off at the gym tonight, I bet.'

She shook her head. 'Pizza.' Mac might like her shape but there was that tight dress to wear to the wedding.

'Hello, Kelli. The family table?' The head waiter gave her a friendly smile.

'If it's available, James. I don't want to put you out.'

'No problem. After you.' He picked up two menus, the wine list, and waved a hand in the direction of their table tucked into a private corner of the spacious restaurant.

After hearing about her parents not being able to come, James removed two of the settings as Kelli and Mac settled into their places.

Mac waved away the wine menu. 'It'll have to be water or something equally innocuous. Kelli?'

'Water for me. And I'll have a margherita pizza.'

Mac placed his order, then sat back to look around at the lunchtime crowd filling the room. 'It's always busy in here.'

'And noisy. The food's fun, the atmosphere's fun.' The company was fun. Though after that revelation about his wife Kelli no longer felt she was on a date with Mac. She didn't know what she felt, but that excitement had evaporated.

'Relax and enjoy, Kelli. I didn't mean to spoil our time together.'

'How do you know what I was thinking?'

'You have a very expressive face. Especially when you're not with patients you're trying to keep details from.'

'I hate the bad stuff. I couldn't be the doctor giving people awful news. It's hard enough helping them after they've learned it, but I like being there to help them through it.'

'That's why you make a great nurse. And I doubt it stops there.'

Maybe this was still a date of sorts. It sure was starting to feel like one again. Keep the compliments flowing and for the next hour she'd sideline her determination to enjoy Mac from a distance.

'Hello, Kelli,' boomed her father from above her.

'Dad! You're joining us for lunch? I thought Mum cancelled.' Disappointment at not having Mac to herself warred with happiness and trepidation.

'Your mother wasn't cancelling my lunch with my girl and her new man.' Dad turned to Mac with his hand out. 'I'm Dale Barnett, Kelli's father as you've probably gathered.'

Mac stood and took the outstretched hand to shake. 'Pleased to meet you. I'm Mac Taylor.'

'Sit down, sit down.' Her father pulled out a chair beside her, and directly opposite Mac, no doubt to observe him. 'You two work together, then?'

'Yes, we do,' Mac agreed. 'The dreaded night shift.'

'Lots of quiet time to hide away in storerooms together?'

'Dad,' Kelli protested. 'It's not like that.'

Both men stared at her, one amused and one, Mac... wistful?

'The emergency department's always busy,' she muttered. Nearly always.

'There are times...' Mac stopped when she ramped up her glare to I-will-kill-you-if-you-keep-going. He shrugged. 'Just—you know.'

Playing his role to its full potential? Regret floored her. She wanted to hide away in a tiny room at work with Mac and kiss him till she couldn't breathe. Wanted, wanted, *wanted* it. But it wasn't happening outside her imagination, an imagination that was only operating to keep the hoax up to speed. 'Mac's head of ED. He has to be super careful.'

Her dad did a mean eye-roll, one she'd known all her life and it always made her laugh. Today was no exception. 'You are my *father*. Not my girlfriend. I'm shutting up about now.' She gave an exaggerated shudder.

Mac was watching them both with amusement all over his face. He really did relax more when he was away from work. Or could be it was when he was with her? She wasn't sure which, but was more than happy to see him like this.

Their meals arrived, including her father's usual carbonara. 'Wine?' he asked.

'Not when I'm working in a couple of hours' time, thanks, Dad.'

'Likewise, Dale.'

'Then I'll just order a glass for me.' He nodded at the waiter before turning back to them. 'How long have you two been going out?'

First question and they hadn't prepared for it. As Kelli floundered for an answer Mac spoke up. 'Since Tamara and Conor's wedding.'

She locked her gaze on him and nodded. Smart. True in a warped way. 'Guess the romance of the occasion got to us.'

Mac leaned back in his chair, his eyes flaring. Hadn't thought of that, had he? 'Yeah,' he drawled.

Kelli couldn't take her eyes off him. When flustered, he was adorable. Gone was that haughty I-am-always-in-control thing, replaced with apprehension and possibly excitement. He was getting to her in more ways than she'd have imagined. And didn't need.

Dad cleared his throat. 'Hate to interrupt, but your food's getting cold.' Meaning he wanted to talk.

Heat swamped her cheeks, and there was a reciprocal colour going on in Mac's too. 'Sorry,' she muttered.

'Don't,' warned Mac softly.

'Don't what?' Oh, sorry. 'Got it.' She'd been working at keeping that word off her tongue but embarrassment had got in the way.

'You okay with the lift-off time arranged for you on Friday?'

Thank you, Dad. Keep it simple and we'll get through lunch unscathed. 'No problem.'

She should've known better than to think unscathed. This was the man who'd known her from the moment she arrived in the world. 'You're booked into one of the front suites overlooking the beach. Secluded for when you want to get away from the crowd.'

Dad. 'Err, thanks.'

Mac was pressing his lips together, as if he was smothering a smile. 'We're very appreciative, Dale. Aren't we, Kelli?'

Mac. 'Err, yes.'

Mac pushed back his chair and stood up. 'Excuse me.'

Kelli watched him head to the men's room, thinking she wanted to strangle him for leaving her to deal with her father's amusement. 'I suppose it's time to leave. I've got heaps to do before I go to work.'

'I like him,' Dad said. 'A lot.'

Trouble was stirring. 'You hardly know him.'

'I make instant decisions every day of my working life. I am good at reading people. Your Mac is an excellent man.' Dad rose and tugged her up onto her feet and into a familiar hug. 'I'm pleased for you.'

Tears threatened and she had to blink hard to prevent the spill-over. 'I'm pleased too.' She meant that. When she shouldn't.

'How serious are you?'

'We're engaged.' Agh! Where did that come from? Being with someone she was never on edge around had its downside.

Dad leaned back to stare at her. 'You are? When were you going to tell us?'

'After the wedding.' Liar. 'Or maybe on Friday at the family dinner. We didn't want to steal the show from Billy.'

'This isn't a bit sudden?' The hug was over, the mood serious. Not that hugs weren't serious in her family, but they interfered with straight questions and answers in Dad's book. 'You might've got together at Tamara's wedding but since then you've spent most of your time in Fiji.'

Nothing but love and concern stared out at her from those

faded blue eyes. Eyes that rarely missed a trick. 'You're not doing this to spite Jason?'

Absolutely. 'No. Please start believing me.'

'How sure of your feelings for Mac are you?'

She got brave. 'The first time you met Mum how did you feel?'

'Baffled, bemused, and… I'm not telling my daughter what I was feeling.'

'Touché.'

'That's how you feel about Mac?'

'I'm not telling my father.' She wasn't even admitting it to herself. Not much.

Dad chuckled. 'Then I'm happy for you. Your mum's going to be ecstatic.'

'Don't rush us. I want to enjoy this one day at a time.' Her heart slowed. Now she seemed to be believing her own lies. Even a faux engagement to Mac was proving to be intriguing and exciting, and she was beginning to wonder how she'd walk away from it. No walking away from Mac though. He'd be in her life every day, every shift, every visit to the gym—though she could change that. Male and pine scent would be in the air she breathed. Mac induced heat under her skin. No, not that close. Yes, that close. Grr. Now she'd have to fight harder to keep her distance.

'Love you, baby girl.' Those comforting arms returned, winding around her shaking body and holding her against that familiar, to-go-to-in-moments-of-pain chest that had been a part of her whole life.

Tears leaked down her face. What a mess. Breathing in, she dug deep for composure. It was all a lie and she'd told it to this man who'd always had her back. 'It's okay.'

Then Dad was letting her go and turning around. 'Mac, I hear congratulations are in order.' He slapped Mac on the shoulder in that way guys did these things and nodded. 'I'm thrilled at the news.'

Mac shot her a startled glance, then quickly recovered. 'Thank you, Dale. I'm only sorry we've kept quiet about this, but Kelli was concerned about spoiling her brother's big day.'

'I'm going to tell your mother the moment I get back to the office. Teach her for letting all those little wedding details keep her running around like a headless chook.' He was grinning like the toddler with ice cream. 'I'm so going to love this. Payback for when I had to miss Billy and Leanne telling her last week they're pregnant.'

'They're pregnant?' Wow. 'That's wonderful, brilliant. I'm going to be an auntie? When?'

'Some time in September.' His chest was expanding with pride. 'The next generation begins.'

Mac dropped an arm over Kelli's shoulders. 'Is this to be kept secret until after the wedding?'

Could divert interest off them.

'I shouldn't have mentioned it but the excitement of your news got to me. Keep it between yourselves, will you?' Her father didn't look at all contrite.

'Of course.' If only she could say the same about their engagement. But a baby? The first in their generation. Awesome. *Go, Billy.* Then her heart flip-flopped as if it were in thick mud. A baby. Would she ever get the chance to have one, to be a mum?

Her eyes slid sideways, drank in the man talking to Dad while watching her too closely. She'd found a great man for the dad role.

Flip, flop.

Her heart ached through its sluggish moves.

She'd made a colossal mistake involving Mac in the

weekend. She just couldn't do it. She would have to back out, tell her parents it was all wrong and that she'd lied.

Running away from Mac wasn't going to change what was going on in her head. Forget her head. If she'd relied on that there'd be no problem. No, her heart was to blame for making such a botch-up of a simple plan. It—all right, *she* was falling for the tall, enigmatic man who'd stood by her all week and seemed more than ready to go as far as it took to make her weekend enjoyable.

Six weeks working in Fiji hadn't calmed the simmering in her veins. Perhaps she should apply for twelve months on base in Antarctica. Except personnel were usually sent south in late spring, not mid-autumn. She'd have to come up with another plan to save her heart. If she wasn't already too late.

CHAPTER SIX

KELLI CLICKED THE safety harness into place, silently cursing herself for not finding a way out of the weekend, and gazed out over the harbour. An offshore breeze had the water skipping as it pushed towards the downtown wharves. 'We do live in a beautiful city,' she murmured in Mac's direction.

'I agree.' Sitting next to her, he appeared relaxed despite two of her brothers and their wives also on board the flying machine. The family had heard the news, and Andy and Phil had been giving Mac the eye from the moment they showed up at the helipad. Mac had been holding her hand until they'd boarded, no doubt to add authenticity to their relationship.

Validation or not, she'd been more than happy to go along with it since it meant having those long, strong fingers entwined with hers. Meant feeling his palm pressed against hers, heat radiating up her arm and tightening her belly. And bringing pictures of a large bed to mind. Was she sex-starved, or what?

Sitting so close her thigh was touching Mac's, she fought the urge to grab his hand again. *Pretend you hate flying.* As if. One big fib was one too many. She wasn't about to start telling more to anyone, and especially not to Mac. He'd stepped up to the mark for her when he didn't have to and somehow not being totally honest would undermine her feelings for him. There was an idea. Put the kibosh on her ever-increasing awareness of him.

Then Mac reached over and took her hand in his again, slid those fingers she adored back into place. More authenticity? Or was he by any chance feeling the same need as her? No answer to that—because she wasn't going to ask. That would be laying too much on the line, and at the moment there was still time to pull back, withdraw entirely, be remote over the weekend. Remote when they were sharing a suite, *with* a double bed? Remote negated the whole purpose of Mac partnering her.

Remember the rules. That shouldn't be hard, knowing Mac was still grieving. Except sometimes she felt he forgot that and enjoyed himself.

The helicopter shook as the rotors wound up to speed, and everything vibrated as they left the ground behind and rose into the blue sky. Tiny puffs of white cloud lightened the blue, made it pretty. Kelli loved flying, had even contemplated getting a private licence but put it in the 'too hard' basket because of the hours required to train and all the exams that had to be sat.

'You're enjoying this, aren't you?' Mac had leaned close so as she could hear him.

Breathing deep to take in that smell of pine and something else she couldn't put her finger on except that it was uniquely Mac, she nodded. 'It's a great way to start what's going to be a fantastic weekend.' Fingers crossed.

Below and to the right the volcanic Rangitoto Island stood proud against the backdrop of sea. Not extinct but in a slumberous state, the iconic double-coned shape looked inviting. Not frightening. Bit like the approaching weekend. Approaching? It had already started. There was no going back now.

When they walked into their suite, Kelli was sure that there was no way she would ever get her fingers to straighten again. She had to force her hand away from Mac's as she scoped the classy room. Fantastic was only the beginning. The room's full-length glass doors opened onto a small deck overlooking the beach and the expansive Waitemata Harbour beyond with the outlying islands and innumerable pleasure craft criss-crossing the sparkling waters.

That was only the view. There was the man who'd walked beside her from the helipad to the resort's reception and on to their room, laughing at her brothers' cheeky taunts and not letting a thing frazzle him.

Then there was that super-king-sized bed dominating the centre of the room they'd be sharing for two days— and two nights. 'Mac, this is all a mistake,' she whispered.

Not so quiet he didn't hear. 'Want me to hitch a ride back when the helicopter returns to the city for more guests?' A wistful note had entered his voice, softened his mouth. 'I can if you want me to.'

'It would've been easier if we'd been given a shoebox-sized room with grotty furnishings and a view of the other side of the resort building's back wall.'

'No romance factor?'

Kelli's head dipped in acknowledgement. 'It all seemed so easy back in the city.' Spreading her fingers wide, she waved her hand at the scene before them. 'This is real. This has nothing to do with the story I've made up to keep my family off my back.'

Mac caught her shoulders, pulled her closer to him. 'Stay focused, Kelli. Keep reminding yourself why we're sharing this amazing suite. And I'll...' He faltered. Tipped his head back and swallowed hard. 'I'll only do what you ask of me. No more, no less.'

He'd put it back on her. Thanks, Mac. She should be grateful. Only she wasn't. She wanted what they had never planned on, what hovered between them in memories of one hot night after another wedding in another city. If they spent the coming nights in bed making love would she finally get the fizz out of her blood? At last be able to look at Mac and know she didn't want him for ever?

No answers blindsided her. Just the heat from those hands on her shoulders to remind her.

You don't always get what you want in this world.

Or did you?

Get real.

Even when her body was crying out for release, and her head was saying go for it, make the most of the situation, tomorrow was just another day.

But then there was want and there was *want*. She wanted a night with Mac. Wanted to trust him enough to fall completely in love with him. Wanted a future with him that involved the picket fence and two-point-seven kids, or whatever the national average was these days. She did? Yes, a brood of knee-huggers was on her bucket list—once she'd found the right man to have them with.

Tick. Done that.

Shut up, brain.

'Kelli? You're spooking me with that worried look.'

Sorry. Didn't count if she didn't say it out loud. 'I'm fine. Just a few nerves. You haven't seen me like this before. I like to do everything perfectly. I get that from my mum. For a moment there I felt there was a deep chasm I had to cross before everything would work out for me.'

'For us.'

'Us, yes.' Mac was totally here for her. Amazing, and scary. No other man, certainly not her real fiancé, had done that no questions asked. 'Thank you.' Apparently of their own accord her feet lifted her up so her lips could reach Mac's. When her mouth grazed his gently she shuddered with need, and felt a returning movement from Mac. Pressing closer, she opened her mouth, expanded the kiss, and tasted him.

Mac's hands landed on her waist, held her like a fragile package, and kept her from moving closer—or away. His mouth took over the kiss, deepening it, allowing their tongues to tangle. If not for those hands Kelli would've sagged against him, length to length, thighs touching, her breasts pushed against his chest, his growing reaction pressing into her stomach. If not for those blasted hands holding her in place. As though Mac was as uncertain as she was how far to take this.

Kelli froze. 'We have rules in place for this very reason.'

Instantly Mac dropped his hands and stepped back. 'Two minutes in the room and I can't control myself.'

'I think I have to take responsibility. I did start the kiss.' Her body was screaming: more, more. What there was of a brain in her head, and that was up for debate, was shouting, *Get away from him. He's not yours, not your future. Only your date for the weekend.*

'Let's go for a walk on the beach before we join the others at the bar,' Mac suggested.

'Separately. You go left, I'll go right.'

'No can do. We're a couple, remember? Newly engaged at that. I'm thinking those brothers would notice faster than a jet on take-off if we don't do this properly.'

'You're right.' Did properly mean more kisses? *If so, bring it on.*

I am toast. Burnt toast.

Falling for Mac is a huge mistake. He's been married, is still grieving the first one. And those are only his *points against a relationship.* She hadn't the energy to drag up all hers. They'd spoil the weekend—if she hadn't already done that by kissing Mac within moments of walking in here. 'I'll change out of my heels. That sand isn't going to be as forgiving as the promenade at Darling Harbour.'

Mac became busy, unzipping his suit bag and withdrawing two suits to hang in the wardrobe. Shirts followed, jeans and chinos. He hadn't skimped when it came to packing. 'Better hang that dress up,' he commented.

'Good thinking.' She hadn't gone to the trouble of getting it pressed to just leave it lying over the back of a chair in a full-length carry bag. Like Mac, she'd unpack everything now. Anything to keep her distracted from Mr Diversion who was quickly becoming Mr Attraction. Ah ha, could be why he was so intent on emptying his bag too. 'Did you leave anything behind?' she asked when he began to fill a drawer with tee shirts and a jersey and everything a man could need when isolated on an island for a month.

Mac shrugged. 'There was room in my bag so I kept putting clothes in until I couldn't any more.'

'You weren't a Boy Scout, then?'

'No. I don't like being caught short and having to make do.' He looked over at her bag, nearly as large as his, and shook his head at her. 'You weren't one either?'

'As if. Did you leave any hangers for me?' Hotels never provided enough.

'One or two.' Mac grinned. 'Want a water before we hit the beach?' Obviously over that awkward moment.

'I'd better.' Once they reached the bar it wouldn't be water she'd be drinking. Her brothers would make a beeline for the drinks department and line them up as soon as they'd dumped their bags in their rooms. No fussing about hanging clothes for them, though these days their wives didn't let them get away with such behaviour quite so easily.

Mac was opening two small bottles from the fridge, looking relaxed. Looking as if he were on holiday, not in the middle of a family occasion where he knew no one. She'd be uptight and fearful of making mistakes if it were her. Taking a closer look at him, Kelli couldn't find any hint of stress or worry. No, that heart-stopping face was open and happy, so unlike the doctor she worked with. Yes, her heart was doing the stop-start thing as she gazed at him.

Snatching up a light jersey to sling around her shoulders in case the breeze turned chilly, Kelli slugged back some water and aimed for the door. 'Let's go.' The room had become airless and small. At least the beach was wide and long and there'd be lots of fresh air coming in on the light sou'wester.

Mac strolled along the beach, his hands jammed into his pockets, his stance relaxed, his mind anything but quiet. Kelli did this to him. Stirred him up something shocking, tossing possibilities of happiness at him, then knocking reality back in place with her honesty.

Beside him she was chirping away non-stop about incidentals: one of her brothers' passion for rugby, the colour of her outfit for tonight's dinner, her mother's penchant for arriving exactly on time for everything. Kelli was nervous, and it was becoming contagious. Trying to lighten the atmosphere, he said, 'I am house-trained: don't pee on the carpet or hoick my food back up under the table.'

She flipped around so she was walking backwards, annoyance fighting with laughter in her expression. 'I am acting over the top, aren't I?'

'Totally. Why the nerves? You were okay up until we got here.'

And you kissed me in our suite.

Was that the cause of her jumpiness? That kiss had been unexpected, and the perfect antidote to his nervousness. It had loosened the tension that had begun gripping him since they'd gathered with her brothers at the helipad. Not that he had any difficulty with meeting new people and sharing a weekend at a special occasion with them, but the lie he and Kelli were living had hit home when he saw Andy wrap his sister up in a bear hug and get swiped for crushing her new blouse. Family stuff that spoke volumes about love and understanding and didn't need a lie sitting bang in the middle.

As a kid he'd never minded being the only child because it had meant he'd got all his mother's attention. Not that there was a lot going spare after she'd seen to his father's demands. Watching Kelli with her lot, he felt a pang of envy. If he'd had siblings he might've coped a little better with losing Cherie. Not gone off into solitude in an attempt to shut down his feelings. Something he'd achieved all too well. Now it was difficult letting go of the restraints he'd placed on those emotions.

Not when you're around Kelli.

And that was the problem with being here.

Impervious to where his thoughts had gone, Kelli was answering his question in some depth. He focused and tried to catch up.

She was saying, 'You're already fitting in. It's like they've always known you, but don't be fooled. The boys will test you, make sure you're good enough for me. Hardly fair, considering.'

'You want my take on that?' When she nodded, her teeth nibbling her bottom lip, he ignored the cuteness and continued. 'It's good they do that, shows how much they care. And for the record, I can handle whatever they throw at me.'

'You're as cocky as them.'

He winced. Bad word. While his body might appear relaxed there was a lot of tension in certain areas that needed relief—and that wasn't going to happen any time soon, if at all. He hadn't come here with the intention of becoming intimate with Kelli. But if it was on offer how would he be able to turn her down? 'You reckon?'

'Yes, I do.'

'Watch out!'

Too late. Still walking backwards, she hadn't seen the piece of driftwood in the sand. Mac grabbed her before she could trip and fall to the ground. Holding her again. Twice since they'd arrived. His hands burned from the feel of her skin under his palms. Other parts of his anatomy tightened. 'I'm going to sleep on the deck tonight.'

'What?' Cobalt eyes locked on him.

Showed how thrown he was, saying that out loud. Now that he had, he might as well put it all out there. 'If you think I can share that huge bed with you and not touch you, then, lady, you ain't got a clue.'

Kelli stared and stared. The air cracked with heat between them. And still she stared. Then she did that lifting-up-on-her-toes thing and he knew what was coming, and was incapable of stopping her. Didn't even want to.

Those full lips he pretended not to fantasise about brushed his mouth softly, left to right, and her tongue did a slow lap of his lips. A groan ripped out of him. He had to hold her close, to kiss her senseless, to feel her body pulsing against his.

His hands found the edge of her blouse and tugged to

make room to slide up underneath, to caress that hot, silky skin. Her breasts pressed against his chest, her nipples pebbles against his pecs. Driving him insane with need. Tipping him further into the mire he did not want to be in. Yet *had* to be in. It was unavoidable. Kelli did that to him.

Her arms were around his neck, keeping him close as that sweet, tormenting mouth worked magic on him. Kisses weren't meant to knock your knees out from under you.

'Oi, you two, this is a public beach,' Phil called out from a balcony nearby.

Kelli spun out of his hold, her hands caressing as they slid from his neck. 'Great. Now there'll be no end to the teasing.' Her forefinger ran slowly over her lips, touching where his lips had been, as though sealing in the kiss.

Mac fought the urge to take her hand and draw that finger into his mouth, to brush his tongue up and down the length. He won, but only just. His hands remained at his sides in tight fists as he strived for nonchalance. To be seen in a horny state in front of Kelli's brothers would only give her more grief and lead to a weekend of hell. In the nicest possible way.

He ground his teeth and banged on a smile. False, fake, whatever; it was a smile that hopefully said, 'I'm here for your sister and don't dare interfere,' in case Phil could read him across the fifty metres of sand that separated them. Mac nudged Kelli. 'Game face, remember. We've got to act the part or everyone will know.'

Kelli flipped her head back to glare at him, a big, fat question in her eyes. 'That kiss wasn't genuine? You were role playing?' Hurt darkened her words.

Say yes, and he wouldn't even get the deck to sleep on. Say no, and there was a possibility he'd be raising hope in Kelli for something he wasn't prepared to contemplate. Rock or hard place? Try honesty. Then buy a shovel to get out of the mess that'd get him into. 'I only do genuine kisses.'

The glare softened, but didn't completely vanish.

Mac leapt further into the mire. 'When we kiss I forget everything sane and sensible.'

Her mouth dropped open. 'Oh.' That familiar red shade coloured her cheeks and she looked away, out to sea.

Bet she wasn't noticing the water or the boats buzzing past.

Why had he told her she distracted him so much? Because he'd been distracted. Why else? Thing was, what would she do with that gem of information? Toss him off the deck, or send him home when the helicopter returned shortly?

'Mac, I shouldn't have kissed you. Both times. It's my fault we're going to get stick from the family.'

He was off the hook. If he let her take the blame. 'It took both of us to make that kiss so hot. If I hadn't been totally immersed in kissing you I'd have remembered what we agreed to.' It was impossible not to lose himself in her kisses. This was like coming out of a drought and soaking up all available water to the point of saturation. Doubt there was any such thing as too many of Kelli's kisses, but he had to try. 'Let's aim to keep ourselves under control. A little bit anyway.'

'Got any suggestions on how to go about that? Apart from one of us moving to a different resort for the weekend?' The words were sharp but there was confusion in Kelli's beautiful eyes. 'I don't understand. It's as though when we're away from work there's nothing keeping us apart. Like when we were in Sydney.'

Don't mention Sydney.

That night was etched into his brain, right at the front where there was no avoiding it. 'Unfinished business?'

Ouch. 'We didn't want that night to finish.' Until he'd wised up outside her door and left to go to his room alone.

Relief pushed aside whatever else Kelli had been thinking. 'You're right. We've had one amazing time together so naturally we want to do it again. But we can't. We work together now. Imagine how we'd deal with spending eight hours a day in the same department if we repeated ourselves? It would be next to impossible. I'll stop kissing you.'

At least one of them was being rational. Shame it wasn't him. 'You're right.'

He wanted to risk messing with his job? To take Kelli to bed and put up some more memories, then have to see her day in, day out, so close he would know her scent, her voice, her everything? 'Come on. Let's head to the bar and join the rest of your family.'

No amount of challenges or teasing from those guys could be as difficult as this conversation. There were no answers to half the things they were talking or thinking about. He was not in the market for romance. Could not bear the thought of losing someone else even if he had love to spare. Somehow over the coming hours and days he'd have to dig deep and find that remote place he favoured so much. The place that kept his heart safe and his head on the job, not on a lovely, sexy, fun woman.

'The helicopter's back. That means everyone from my family's here. And Jason.'

'Can't wait to meet him,' Mac muttered. Couldn't wait to show him that Kelli was unavailable. For the next few days at any rate.

And then what? When the wedding was done and they'd all returned to Auckland City what would happen between him and Kelli? Would Monday night be the big announcement night?

*Hey, guys, Kelli and I are calling our engagement off.
See you around some time.*

Mac shuddered.

Kelli nudged him with an elbow. Even that was a hot
move. 'You realise this is when we break the news of our
engagement to everybody outside my immediate family? Mum will be expecting it, and Dad will have got the
champagne ready.'

'How did your mother take the news?' Kelli had sent
him a text to say her father had done as he'd said and
spilled the beans. She hadn't said anything else and he
didn't know how to read that.

'She's all over the place with it. Excited to have another
wedding to plan for. Believe me, she gets her thrills from
organising events and people. But then she rang me and
demanded to know why you and not Jason, and gave me
the low-down on all his good points. I can recite them
off by heart. Then her next call was to ask when we want
to get married. How many people we would be inviting.'

'It's going to break her heart when we pull out.'

'No, it won't. She'll carry on, changing one groom for
the other. Win, win. Or should that be lose, lose?'

'You're nibbling your bottom lip again.' Cute and spoke
volumes of her distress. 'Is it okay to hold hands while we
walk in to join everyone?' He wanted to give her secu-
rity, show he was on her side, at her side, had no regrets
about volunteering to be here for her. 'Or is that a bit like
kissing? Too much contact?'

'We're going to drink to our engagement. We're meant
to hold hands.' Nibble, nibble.

He wanted to kiss those lips, gently possess them so
she'd stop gnawing. He couldn't, not if he wanted to keep
the fire roaring through him under control—at least a
little bit.

CHAPTER SEVEN

'BILLY, LEANNE—THIS is Mac Taylor. I'm sure you've heard about him by now.' Kelli bit back on the excitement. If this moment had been for real she wouldn't have been able to contain herself.

Mac and Billy were shaking hands, her brother giving her *fiancé* a thorough going-over.

'Give him a break.' Kelli elbowed Billy.

Leanne gave her infectious laugh. 'Mac, you and I have to talk about the Barnett crowd and how they like to flex their muscles around outsiders. I have a few tips that'll help you contain them.'

Mac gave Leanne a peck on her cheek. 'What are you doing now?'

'About to sip a drop of champagne to celebrate your engagement.' Leanne didn't sound the least put out that this was supposed to be exclusively her night.

But Kelli had to make doubly sure she knew she hadn't deliberately tried to spoil her fun. 'I'm really sorry this got out, Leanne.' Sort of true, though no point going through the whole deal if no one knew. 'We don't want to take anything from your special weekend.'

'Believe me, I'm glad some of the heat's being trans-ferred off us. I'm already feeling overwhelmed, and it's only going to get worse. What if I botch the ceremony? Trip up, or get my words all wrong?'

Kelli slipped her arm through Leanne's. 'Who cares? This is all about you and Billy. He loves you and if you say something not in the script he isn't going to mind. Perfect's highly overrated and boring. Just relax and enjoy the weekend. It's your wedding, not a movie set with a tyrant for a director.'

Leanne sniffed and squeezed her arm tight against Kelli's. 'Thanks, sister-in-law-to-be. You're right, but it's hard to be calm when everyone's rushing around asking have you got this, done that, ready for it all.'

'Go hug Billy,' *and get him away from interrogating Mac.* She nudged Leanne gently. 'He's your rock, and understands what you're going through.'

'You know the right thing to say when people are in a state, don't you?' Mac was back at her side, none the worse for having Billy check him out.

'I try.' Something she'd learned as a youngster dealing with the bullies, and had never stopped doing.

Loud voices and laughter came from the reception area that ran the length of the bar room. Mac stared across the heads. 'I take it that's your mother?'

Kelli didn't need to look. 'That's Mum in full organisational mode. She'll be counting heads, checking who's still in their suite and not here for the first glass of champagne.' Pride filled her. Mum was good at this sort of thing.

'You're a little like that, though a lot quieter,' Mac commented. 'There's no doubting you're related. She's a very good-looking woman.'

The air hissed out of her lungs. How was she supposed to walk away from this man next week? 'You could charm a rattlesnake if you tried,' she gasped.

'Never had the opportunity.' That was all Mac had time for before his hand was grabbed by her mother.

'You must be Mac. Welcome to our weekend.' Mum was doing a fast but thorough perusal of Kelli's fiancé.

'Thank you, Mrs Barnett. I'm happy to meet you all.'

'Then you're a brave man,' her mother said. 'Warning, drop the Mrs Barnett fast. I'm Trish.' Her eyes were still watching him too closely.

Feeling sorry for Mac, Kelli interceded. 'Did you get the crayfish sorted?'

Of course she would have, but for once Kelli was all out of things to say. Having Mac here as her fiancé was making her belly wind tight, and tighter. This was not how she'd ever thought she'd be announcing to the world she'd be getting married. The fact it was a lie only made it worse, and she wanted to call a halt, to tell everyone she'd made a mistake and wipe the untruth away. But once it had been put out there it would never go away. Even when she announced the engagement was off there would be comments and commiserations.

'Hey, Kelli, how are you? I hear you've got some news to share.'

Jason. The moment had arrived. Would he accept it? Or put up a fight? He was smiling that open, friendly way he always did with her. Genuine and caring. Confident and totally misguided.

She was engulfed in a friendly hug. 'Jason, hi.' Then she felt a hand at her back. Mac had stepped up. *Here we go.* This was what the whole deal with Mac was about. Pulling free, she said, 'Jason, I'd like you to meet Mac Taylor.' She couldn't add, 'my fiancé'. She just couldn't.

'Mac.' Like everyone else in her family Jason put his hand out, shook politely. There was the same challenge in Jason's eyes as her brothers had put out there. But not like a jealous man who'd been thwarted in love. *Not making sense here, Jason.*

'Pleased to meet you.' Mac sounded relaxed and unconcerned, but the hand on her back had tensed. 'I hear you're almost one of the family.' Not as much as Mac would be if he actually were to marry Kelli.

Jason nodded, studying Mac thoroughly. 'Dale and Trish have been good to me, probably saved me from going off the rails.' His scrutiny moved to her, but he said nothing more.

Clink, clink. A spoon tapping against a glass quietened the room. 'Listen up, everyone.' Dad to the rescue without knowing he was needed.

Then Kelli realised he was looking around for her and Mac, and her stomach sank. 'Here we go.' Not the right diversion at this moment.

Mac leaned close. 'You're doing great.'

Never had she felt so supported by anyone whose surname was not Barnett. She snuggled a little bit nearer to her rock. 'Are you ready for this?'

'As ready as I'm ever going to be.' His hand found hers, held her firmly.

When Kelli looked at him she fully expected to see a grim expression on his beautiful face. Surprise rattled her. Mac looked happy. Happy? Because they were announcing a fake engagement? Or because he was doing this to help her out of a bind? As she stretched up on her toes he suddenly looked startled. No, she wasn't about to kiss him. 'You're wonderful.'

Delight returned. 'Of course.' He grinned.

'Glasses of champagne are being passed around. When you've all got one I'd like to propose a toast.' Dad was suddenly in front of her and Mac, Mum's arm through his.

A tray appeared before her and Kelli picked up a glass,

not surprised to find her hand was shaking. It still wasn't too late to back out, to admit what she'd done and then go into hiding. Mac squeezed her hand, giving her the confidence to continue.

Looking around at the smiling faces she wanted to believe this was for real. Then she saw Jason. His mouth had flat-lined. No cajoling smile now. She should feel sorry for him, but that emotion wasn't coming to the fore. Instead anger that he'd helped her to take this unusual step began expanding throughout her. Until Mac squeezed her hand again.

Thank goodness for Mac. She'd been about to ruin the evening, especially for her family. Plastering on a smile, she waited for the next instalment of this crazy ride.

Back to Dad. 'This weekend is about Billy and Leanne, and Trish and I are thrilled we're all here to share it with them.' He raised his glass. 'To Billy and Leanne.'

'To Billy and Leanne.' The champagne was delicious. Kelli dipped her head in acknowledgement to her father. He'd done the right thing. She wasn't off the hook, but he'd put her brother first.

Then, 'I've also got some more wonderful news to share.' Dad and Mum moved closer to her and Mac. 'For those of you who haven't met him yet, this imposing man is Mac Taylor, and, as of this week, Kelli's fiancé.'

It was Billy who raised his glass and said, 'To Kelli and Mac.'

Billy, who didn't mind his sister nudging in on his weekend, was grinning at her as he used to when he'd put something horrible and wet and cold in her bed.

Tears spurted out and down her cheeks. Her beloved family might give her a hard time but they were always there for her. As was the man holding her hand and tugging gently. When she looked up into Mac's eyes, her heart broke. It was too much. If only this were for real. She was falling in love with him. Not a doubt lifted, not a question waved at her. But he wouldn't love her back.

'To Kelli and Mac.' The toasts bounced off her, echoing throughout the room, and the tears flowed.

'Hey, come here.' Mac wrapped her in his arms and held her gently.

Laughter broke out and the usual cheeky comments from her brothers added to the good cheer. Kelli shivered. Everyone thought her tears were about her joy. Only Mac knew they weren't and he was sticking to her like glue until her meltdown dried up. She really had given him a lot to deal with. 'Sorry,' she whispered.

'I'm not, okay? It was never going to be easy. Let's take our drinks and go sit at an outside table.'

'We won't be left alone.'

'You don't want to be. That'd look odd.'

'Where did you learn all this stuff?' She gazed at Mac. 'It can't have been in any medical training manual.' And he didn't have siblings.

He laughed. Really laughed, as though there was nothing wrong here. 'You want sensible? I've got loads of it. Too much.' He removed her glass from her fingers. 'Let's get refills and head out into the twilight.'

That would be romantic if only they hadn't just put out a big fat lie to everyone. Kelli sucked in her stomach, straightened her back and went with Mac, acknowledging the good wishes as they moved through her family. They were barely seated when her brothers and their wives joined them. Disappointment warred with common sense. Being alone with Mac would add to her confusion and longing; having the guys here meant putting up with relentless teasing.

Teasing was likely the safer option. She couldn't get into any trouble that way.

* * *

Mac stood up from the table where he'd been seated with Kelli and her brother, Andy, and his wife for dinner. 'Seems we're the last ones left,' he said unnecessarily. There was no further putting off heading to that suite with Kelli. The barman was wiping down the counter and tipping semi-defrosted ice into the sink with a loud clatter.

'Thought you two would've been the first to head to your room.' Andy winked as he too stood.

Kelli slowly unwound her body and came up beside Mac, holding herself rigid.

Mac nudged her softly. Be careful or Andy would notice something wasn't kosher. She nodded and slipped her arm through his. 'Goodnight, you two. See you bright and early for breakfast, Rach. It's going to be full on with hair, nails, and make-up to be done.'

'Let's hope that rain doesn't eventuate. Leanne must be having kittens worrying about that.' Rach was looking through the windows at what was now a gloomy scene.

The ceremony would take place in the gardens, and from what Mac had seen of Trish Barnett the weather had better clear up or she'd create havoc. The woman was a mini-storm all of her own. Something he needed to remember in the coming days. She was not going to let him break up with Kelli easily, if at all. Though she did have a contingency plan—Jason.

The man had sat through drinks and then dinner looking a little stunned, as though he was slowly absorbing the truth about his relationship with Kelli. He didn't appear too upset, more surprised. Probably felt stupid for continuing to try and win Kelli over when it had never been on the cards. Mac couldn't find it in himself to feel too sorry. If Kelli had any feelings for Jason at all then it'd be different, but he'd watched her over the night and she treated the guy no differently from anyone else.

Mac swallowed an inappropriate smile. His earlier guess about Jason being like family had strengthened, which made *him* feel better. About *his* role in this. About his own feelings for Kelli. For every hour he spent with her there was an increasing sense that he might be getting another chance at happiness. Of course, in the hours he wasn't with her the reasons why he was an idiot were easier to hear. Not that he seemed to be taking a blind bit of notice.

From the moment they'd lifted off the ground in the city he'd felt like a different man: free from the past and those locks he'd put on his heart and now stepping into the unknown. Even excited about being amongst this family and their special weekend, certainly eager to be with Kelli for days, not just hours.

'Goodnight,' Kelli muttered and headed in the direction of their suite, striding out with determination. As if she had something to face and get out of the way.

Mac followed, quickly catching up. 'I mightn't be sleeping on the deck if those showers arrive.'

'You reckon?' The face she tipped up to him was strained and her smile tired.

'I could try the floor.'

'We've got this far—we can manage the rest.' Her mouth stretched into a yawn. 'What have you guys got planned for tomorrow while the females get glammed up?'

'A round of golf.'

'Can you play?'

'I can swing a club, and someone uttered the word "challenge".'

'And you can't turn one of those down.' She paused, giving him the once-over. 'You fit in so well it's scary.'

Pride puffed out his chest, then reality flattened it

again. 'I'm not meant to fit in. These are the men who are going to come after me when you tell them I've dumped you.'

'I'm not going to say that.'

Really? He was in with a chance? But did he want one? He wouldn't have put up his hand to help Kelli out if going their separate ways afterwards hadn't been the conclusion to their engagement. Would he? This was starting to feel more about helping himself, not Kelli. Not only Kelli.

She flashed her entry key at the door pad and shouldered the door open, stepped inside and came to a halt, staring at that enormous bed.

Mac walked past her, trying not to let any X-rated thoughts push aside what little reason lurked in his skull. Continuing to the doors opening onto the deck, he slid one open, peered out and swallowed the need clawing up his throat, tightening *all* of his body. 'Please don't kick me out tonight.'

When Kelli didn't answer he turned to face her. A breath stuck halfway between his lungs and his nose. She was gazing at him with sadness in those cobalt eyes. 'Kelli?' he whispered. 'What's up?'

She blinked, shook away that look. 'Wishful thinking, that's all.' Dropping her clutch purse on a bedside table, she stared around the room, before her gaze came back to him. 'You okay?'

If he didn't want what he couldn't have, then yes, he'd say he was in top form. The air was getting tight, the walls closing in on him. Three steps and he'd be close enough to raise his arms and hug this distracting woman, or kiss her, or pick her up and carry her to that bed to lie together and make love. But that sadness in her eyes had wrought havoc with his emotions. He needed to lighten the mood, to wipe away that despondency. Sex might do the trick, but if Kelli wasn't in the mood then he'd be adding to her problems. 'I'm good. Let's try to get some sleep. I imagine tomorrow's going to be full on for you. Lying back while someone paints your nails. Drinking coffee—or will that be wine?—as your hair's styled and your warpaint applied. Definitely a massive day ahead. Then there's the wedding. With tears.'

She'd cried at Tamara and Conor's wedding.

'The reception dinner with speeches and lots of laughter, the dancing with your brothers and fiancé.' He slapped his forehead. 'Why are you standing there and not rushing to get into your pyjamas?' Another slap. 'I forgot to bring my racing car PJs.'

Kelli's mouth was a startled O. 'Thank goodness for something.' Then she started to laugh. 'You're mad. You know that? At least I don't have to try and hit a tiny ball into a tinier hole a hundred metres down the lawn, and then have to shout a round of top-shelf drinks because I missed hitting the ball in the first place.'

It was good to hear that laughter. It warmed him right to his toes. Tomorrow, fingers crossed, he'd ramp it up when he beat the pants off her brothers. Unless they were top-class golfers, and from the few comments made at dinner he doubted it. 'You want the bathroom while I turn down the covers?'

The bed had already been turned down, but Mac intended being in his side well before she returned from doing whatever took females a lifetime in the bathroom.

'Don't touch my chocolate while I'm in there,' Kelli warned as she pointed at the confections on the bedside tables.

'You won't eat yours.' She was particular about what she put in that delectable mouth. Didn't seem to eat bad food ever.

'I might, after tomorrow.' Kelli rummaged in her case and pulled out some red satin creation. 'But then again, I know what's on the menu for the dinner and I probably won't eat again for a week after that.'

'Kelli, why are you so fixated with what you eat? You're not overweight, not even a tiny bit, so there must be another reason.' His hands had fitted perfectly over her curves when he'd held her earlier, curves that filled his palms with heat, turning him on fast.

Her eyes popped wide, like bugs caught in headlights. 'I'm not exactly svelte.'

'Svelte? Isn't that another word for skinny?'

'Mac, don't. Please.'

Crossing to where she stood, looking as if she was ready to run if he said the wrong thing, Mac lifted a stray strand of hair from her cheek and slipped it behind her ear. The only thing he could say was the truth. 'In my book, you're perfect. Ten out of ten. Beautiful, inside and out.'

A lone tear slowly slid down her cheek. 'That's the nicest thing any man has ever said to me.'

Nice? Blah word that it was, he got her sentiment. And the atmosphere was getting heavy again. So, deep breath, and a quick slap on her bottom. 'Go clean off the warpaint and get into whatever that red outfit is.' It had better be a sack with drawstrings at each end to prevent any access for his hands. The night was going to be one of the longest of his life, and there'd been some doozies in the past.

Only her bedside light was on when Kelli slipped out of the bathroom, her light robe wound tight around her. She should've gone shopping for a winceyette nightgown that reached her ankles, not packed this little number. She hadn't been thinking about the nightwear, only what to bring for the days and evenings right down to the last G-string.

Mac was lying on the edge of the far side, his hands behind his head, and a wobbly smile aimed at her.

Thump-thump. Her heart was cranking up the tempo at the sight of the man she had to share the bed with. Share, but not touch. Rule number one. How did she manage that? There wouldn't be much sleeping going on for sure, and tomorrow she was going to look awful. 'Don't roll over or you'll fall out of bed,' she warned and gave him a quick smile.

'I did mention sleeping on the floor.'

Talk about hopeless. Here she was about to climb into bed with Mac, the guy who had a short while ago told her she was not fat, and who she had started falling for: and nothing was meant to happen.

Nothing's going to happen.

A strangled laugh broke free of her tense body. 'We're crazy,' she spluttered.

Mac grinned at her. 'Absolutely crazy.'

Still laughing, she slid under the cover and switched the light off, plunging the room into complete darkness. 'I'm glad you agreed to do this.'

The mattress moved as he rolled onto his side to face her. 'You had a problem, I had a solution.'

'No regrets?' She held her breath and tried to see his expression in the dim light beginning to push into the room from behind the curtains.

But his face was in shadow. 'Not for a moment.'

She wanted to believe him—she really did. 'A weekend with strangers who are happy to give you a hard time and no regrets? Think I've said it before—you're crazy.'

'That's me.' He laughed softly. 'It's odd but I'm starting to feel alive again. As though I belong somewhere. Not that I'm saying I'm becoming a part of your family. I know that's not on the cards, but they're so friendly and easy to be around that I forget our relationship isn't for real.'

It could be, if he meant what he was saying. 'I suppose that's why you're so convincing.' To the others, not her, though there had been moments when she'd wondered if he did want to be with her. As in properly, completely, every day, with her. 'I'm glad for you. Could be this weekend helps you as much as me.'

'Kelli, can I make love to you? I know it wasn't meant to be, but I want you so much. You make me feel again, to want things I thought I'd never want again.' He wasn't reaching for her, no touch to soften her, tempt her, if she wanted to say no.

Rules one, two and three. No touching or kissing in bed. No sex anywhere.

Rules are made to be broken, repeated that annoying voice in her head.

If they made love then they'd do it again tomorrow night, and it would be harder to walk away from the relationship next week. On the other hand, she was halfway to being in love with Mac and resisting him was nigh on impossible. When her blood was fizzing, muscles tightening in anticipation, and desire winding up fast. She could make and store up exquisite memories for the long, lonely nights to come. Besides, she wanted to give back something to him, and if making him feel alive again was it then she was more than happy. 'Yes,' she sighed around a lump in the back of her throat. 'Please.'

'Don't move.' Mac tossed the covers aside and came over to her. His fingers traced a line from beneath her earlobe to her breast, followed by his lips, soft and tantalising.

When Kelli placed her arms around his neck Mac gently pushed them away. 'Lie back and enjoy.'

'But I want to touch you, to rub you, make you come.'

'Trust me, you're doing that in spades.' His mouth returned to her nipple and with one hot flick her back was arching as need sparked through her.

How? She hadn't done anything. Mac's hands touched her as though with wonder. *Her.* Amazing…

'You're beautiful,' he whispered against her breasts.

She tensed. He couldn't see her properly in the semi-dark.

'I mean it,' he growled against her skin, sending shivers of heat through her.

To hell with not touching him. It was agony, and ecstasy. It was wonderful and frustrating and oh… 'Do that again.'

Her body was shattering as a conflagration of desire and love rolled through her, took her out of this world and shut her mind down, leaving her free to absorb the wonder of Mac's lovemaking.

And then he was above her, entering her, taking her to a whole new level of wonder, going with her, until they both peaked and the heat exploded around, through, between them.

Breaking the rules wasn't so bad.

CHAPTER EIGHT

KELLI HADN'T STOPPED smiling since Mac made love to her last night, and everyone was noticing.

'You two are hot together.' Leanne grinned as they walked into the salon where they were to be made beautiful. 'I've never seen you so happy.'

Mac had told her she was beautiful and she'd begun to go with it. To trust him on this. He hadn't turned away from her that morning when they'd woken in full daylight, he hadn't studied her like a specimen to be catalogued, or the night before's mistake. No scalpels in sight. Instead Mac had reached for her and caressed her before making love with her again. He'd made them late for breakfast and earned a whole load of witty comments from her obnoxious brothers. Mac was in for a long morning on the golf course unless he managed to shut them down.

'I hope those men don't wear themselves out playing golf. Especially Billy. He's going to need his stamina for the wedding and the wedding night.' Kelli poked Leanne on the arm. *Back at you.*

The bride-to-be only laughed. 'No worries on that score.' Then she stopped and hugged Kelli. 'As long as you're happy, that's all anyone wants.'

Her heart stuttered. This wasn't how it was meant to go. The crash was going to hurt a lot more than she'd expected. But then she'd never meant to make love with Mac, or to find herself falling for him. 'I am,' she managed around her doubts. If it were all true then she'd be crazy happy, not just warily perched on cloud nine. Next time Tamara had any insane suggestions like asking Mac to accompany her to something, she'd hang up and stay hung up. Not that it had been her friend's idea to fake an engagement; that brainwave lay entirely with Mac.

But if she'd ignored Tamara she'd have missed out on getting close to Mac, last night being the icing on the cake so far. Tonight might lead to an even sweeter topping. Then tomorrow would come and they'd continue the charade but on Monday reality would strike and the show would be over. Her stomach cramped. Her mouth dried. No. She didn't want that. But perhaps Mac did. He'd signed up for a weekend, not a lifetime. By his own admission this was his first foray back into the dating world. Apparently she had a lot to do with his willingness to participate, but he'd be wanting to test the waters, try out other offerings.

What if she made him fall in love with her? Was that even possible? Where to start?

'Kelli, my girl, don't stand there looking lost.' Mum was at her side. 'You're up for nails first.'

Was this a sign? An answer to her question? Get made to look more than her best, starting with her nails? Be so alluring Mac couldn't resist her. It was a start, and the only one she could come up with. Though it did reek with falseness. Shallow. Not how she wanted any relationship she was involved in to go. She knew first-hand the downside to that. But striving to look fabulous so as to deflect Mac seeing the real her was being honest to herself in a way. Though she was meant to be toughening up about that, it was hard to stop hiding behind amazing clothes and hairstyles and sometimes even witty conversation. Incredible how many people bought it, saw only what she wanted them to.

Mac's not like that.

Could explain her feelings for him. But it'd be a big step to trust him never to see her faults.

'Kelli, you're daydreaming.'

'Yes, Mum.' Sinking onto the chair being held out for her by the nail technician, she smothered a wry smile. If only she were truly engaged and could enjoy the moments of excitement like Leanne, but since she couldn't she'd make the most of the day and have some fun, maybe even figure out how to make Mac think twice about walking away next week.

She could try just being herself. There was a novel idea, and it fitted with being strong.

The hour of the wedding ceremony sped towards Kelli so fast she thought she'd never be ready in time. With chaos surrounding her Leanne had become cool and calm, organising her best friend into the bridesmaid dress and not panicking when some buttons popped off. Kelli took over there, reattaching them with needle and thread after realigning others to allow a bit more room so the dress wasn't quite as tight.

When Kelli went to get dressed in her specially made teal silk shift Mac was nowhere to be seen. His suit was gone so she presumed he'd already showered and dressed and was with the guys somewhere. She swallowed her disappointment at not preparing alongside him. That was what couples did; not them. To be fair, she'd left him with the brothers for most of the day so couldn't expect him to be hanging around waiting for her when she chose to make an appearance. They'd managed lunch together, along with most of the family: a rushed meal with people coming and going, grabbing sandwiches and coffee to have on the run.

Andy had come over when Mac was with her to say, 'Don't believe this one whenever he says he's not good at something. He aced the golf.'

Mac had looked the picture of innocence as he'd said, 'I don't recall saying I wasn't any good at golf.'

Not those exact words, no. 'You did kind of imply it,' she'd laughed before devouring a small salad. This getting glammed up was hard work.

Kelli had just slipped into her dress when the door to the suite opened and Mac strolled in, looking divine in his dark grey evening suit and white shirt. 'Oh, my.'

'Have I got grease on my chin?' The hunk grinned.

She fixed him a look that said 'don't fool with me', and growled, 'Can you do up my zip?' How like a couple that sounded. 'Would you mind?'

'No, I'd hate it.' He was still grinning, which took the edge off what he'd said.

'Then I'll pop down the hallway and knock on the next door to find someone else to help me.'

'Oh, no, you won't,' he growled back. 'While we're a couple, that's my job.' He stepped behind her and sucked in a breath.

While we're a couple. A thrill shivered through her. Mac wasn't touching her zipper. 'Problem?'

A gentle tug where the zip started, then zilch. Only the sensation of kisses whispering over the skin between her shoulder blades. 'Mac.' She had no idea if she said his name out loud, no idea of anything except those kisses caressing her, of whispers of breath as his mouth caressed her skin. 'Mac. Please.'

'Please what?' he asked quietly beside her ear.

Tipping her head back, she felt his lips moving slowly

up her neck, tasting her, awakening her, tightening her belly and creating a tsunami of need centred at her core. 'Take me.'

His laugh was low and sexy and intensified everything she was feeling. 'And have your mother banging down the door asking why we're not already waiting in the ceremony garden? No, Kelli, this is something to be going on with until tonight.'

Mac said that? Nothing like his usual measured speech and words, more like a hot man in need of getting close and personal—with her. Twisting around in his arms her hip swept across his need, rock hard and pushing the front of his trousers out of shape. What was going on? Apart from lust? Did Mac want more too? More likely now he'd got back in the saddle he'd be unable to stop. There was a drought of four years to make up for. Kelli shuddered as if a bucket of icy water had been dumped on her.

Knock, knock. 'Kelli, Mac, are you in there?' Dad called from the hallway.

'What did I tell you?' Mac grinned. 'Trish has sent the cavalry. I'm in the bathroom until Dale's gone.'

'Good idea,' Kelli muttered, glancing at the evidence of his need. 'But first, my zip?'

Nothing sensual about the way Mac dealt with it this time; up and closed, done deal, and her skin was bereft.

Opening the door, she gasped. 'Hey, Dad, what's up?'

'Your mother needs you. Something to do with her jacket not sitting right.' Dad glanced around. 'Where's Mac? He's not gone down already?'

'He's in the bathroom.' She slipped her arm through her father's. 'Come on. Let's go sort Mum out.'

'We can wait for Mac. It's nothing urgent, just Trish flapping in panic with nothing to do. She's so organised, every box ticked twice, nothing going wrong, I swear she's made this crisis up because she can't deal with quiet time.'

Wait for Mac? Kelli could feel laughter beginning to unleash inside. She'd be waiting for ever. 'Mac,' she called and swallowed. 'You going to be long? We're waiting for you.' If only she could see his face. It'd be a picture for sure.

The bathroom door cracked open. 'Nearly ready,' Mac said in such a normal I-am-in-control voice that she had to wonder if there weren't two Macs hanging out in the bathroom.

'That was quick.' The devil had got her tongue. When his eyes widened, she laughed. And then turned away to distract her father. Just in case all was not quite 'ready'.

Of course Kelli cried when Leanne walked down the petal-strewn path towards Billy and the marriage cele-brant. She cried as her brother said his vows, and when he slid the ring onto Leanne's finger. It would've been rude not to when there were tears tracking down Billy's cheeks too. Mac kept handing her tissues from what seemed like a never-ending supply in his pockets. With his other hand he held one of hers, fingers laced, and his thumb rubbing circles on her skin.

'I'll need to find the make-up artist for a repair job soon,' she murmured as she mopped up yet more tears. These ones were for what might have been if only she and Mac were for real.

Mac's fingers squeezed hers. 'You don't need make-up.'

'What is it about weddings that makes me cry? It's not something I go around doing much.'

'You're happy for Billy and Leanne. And…' he leaned

closer '...you're not the only one. There's hardly a dry-eyed female around here.'

'And Dad.' An emotional man, her father, not afraid to show his feelings. 'Third and last son married off.'

'The focus on you is going to be turned up something awful.' Mac stared at her for a long moment.

'What?'

He shook his head. 'Nothing.'

Kelli stood up. 'I'm going to kiss my new sister-in-law then get us some champagne.' She wasn't going to waste time and a wonderful day worrying what was behind that look. Plenty of time once she was back in Auckland to try unravelling what went on in that craggy head focused on her.

For the dinner Mac sat with Kelli at the family table in front of the wedding party. The food was divine, the speeches heart-wrenching at times and hilarious at others. He couldn't remember the last time he'd been so relaxed amongst people who twenty-four hours ago had been strangers. When he and Cherie got married there'd only been a handful of friends and relatives, and while it had been wonderful there hadn't been this amazing family atmosphere.

Dale and Trish had accepted him as Kelli's fiancé and all her brothers had gone out of their way to make him welcome. Which meant trying to catch him out with questions about his past, and challenging him to a game of darts—blindfolded. As for that golf, thank the lucky stars his game had been on. The guys would never have let him live it down if he'd lost to them.

It was all fun and friendly, not a hint of unacceptance. It threatened to drag him in; to tempt him to make this a permanent arrangement; to let go the past and aim for a future. With the gorgeous and loving woman sitting beside him, her hand on his thigh. Possessively? Or lovingly? Or what?

Leaning back in his chair, he covered Kelli's hand with his, felt her jerk as though she hadn't realised what she'd been doing. Pressing down gently, he kept her from withdrawing. He liked her touch, liked that she was happy to be seen touching him. This wasn't a game, wasn't for show to underline their engagement. Kelli had acted impulsively and that stirred him deeply, suggested he might be able to move on some day. Was already easing out of the gloom.

Pulling the brakes back on his emotions was impossible right now. He wanted to let loose a bit, and plain old enjoy a weekend with a woman without having to worry about what tomorrow might bring. As though someone had lifted the shutters on his grief and light had spilled in to banish the darkness. Monday would be the end of this so he might as well grab today and tomorrow with both hands and have a blast. Which included giving Kelli a good time. She deserved it, and he was happy to oblige.

'Up to dancing?' Kelli leaned in to ask, teasing his senses with the smell of roses.

'Now there's a loaded question.' The band had started up a few minutes ago and already the dance floor was heaving. He stood up, tugging Kelli with him, still holding her hand. He never wanted to let her go again.

But he would. He had to. She needed someone she could trust to watch her back. Someone like Jason. That man was perfect for her. Her parents hadn't done her a disservice trying to convince her to date him. Not once since they'd all arrived on Waiheke had he been rude or nasty to him, or Kelli. He'd taken their engagement on the chin like a real bloke.

Kelli was moving to the music as though she'd invented

dancing. Her long body swaying and her hips gyrating, her head tipped back so those dark blonde waves of hair fell down her back.

Mac went with her, his moves matching hers. His mouth was dry and his gut tight. Keep this up and he'd need to take her to the beach before the music stopped. Kiss her senseless, make love to her behind the trees like a crazed teen, hear her groan with pleasure. Come to think of it, he felt like a teen who'd just discovered sex. No slow reawakening for him. Instead wham, bam, can we do it again? He'd gone from low, low, low to a searing high.

There was only one way to go after that.

The band had packed up, the bride and groom had left for their suite, and some of the guests were sitting around the tables leisurely drinking more champagne while they talked and laughed the night away.

Mac and Kelli went for a stroll along the beach, hand in hand, Kelli's shoes swinging from the fingers of her free hand. 'It's good to see Billy so happy,' she said. 'There've been times when none of us believed he'd ever be again.'

Mac felt a hitch in his chest. 'What do you mean?'

'Like you he is, was, a widower.'

The hitch became an ache. 'No one's said a word all weekend.'

'Why would we? Everyone knows about it, no one wanted to blight his and Leanne's special day. Billy has moved on, found happiness again, but I know he hasn't forgotten Carla. Why would he? Why should he? They were a couple in love when life took a tragic turn. Carla would've been the first person to kick his butt and tell him to get on with being happy.'

'What happened?' There was a blockage in Mac's throat impeding his words, flattening them.

'They'd been at Billy's rugby club Christmas party and he'd had too much to drink so Carla drove them home. It was a wet night and she took a corner too fast, spun out and slammed into a power pole.'

Game over. Mac could feel Billy's pain. 'Bet he felt guilty about not being able to drive.'

Kelli nodded as understanding filled her eyes. 'You'd know about that. The guilt, I mean.'

'Yeah.' The word sighed out of him. 'Totally.'

'Want to talk about it?'

Strangely, he did. Which was a first, apart from Tom. Not even his mother had been able to get a word about Cherie's death. 'Cherie had an aneurism.'

Kelli squeezed his fingers and kept walking. 'That made you feel guilty how?'

Not he shouldn't be guilty, but why. 'I'm a doctor.'

'She'd had symptoms? There usually aren't any for an aneurism.'

'I should've known something was wrong. I didn't. Not a whisper, not a hint. I had come home late and Cherie was already in bed asleep.' Tipping his head back, he stared up at the stars, swallowing the pain. 'I remember feeling relieved I could slide in beside her, tuck my arm around her waist, and give into the exhaustion overwhelming me.' He'd been working horrendous hours as he studied for his final exam in emergency medicine and did the days and nights in ED. 'The alarm woke me. Not Cherie. She was gone. According to the autopsy report she'd died about three hours before I woke up. How could I not have known?' The despair, guilt, the anguish all poured out of him in that last question. 'How?' They'd been so connected, so in touch with each other, loved and understood one another so well. 'How?' he cried at the stars.

Kelli's arms wound around him, held him tight. Her

head was tucked against his shoulder, her mouth quiet, her body supple and giving.

Mac breathed deep, drawing in Kelli's scent. Kelli's. The rose fragrance stirred him, reminded him of other things that used to be a part of his life. His family history, the home he grew up in, the laughter whenever Dad was away, the love, the anger. The good and bad. There'd been difficult times, days when he'd nearly run away out of fear of his father, yet he'd stayed because of his mum. Stayed and survived to go on to become a successful doctor, to marry a wonderful woman—and lose her. His heart banged against his ribs. He should've known Cherie was unwell. He'd survived that. If being wary and holding onto his heart and not wanting to get involved with anyone for fear of not being able to protect them, save them, was survival.

Slowly, slowly Kelli's warmth moved into him, heating the cold that had settled around his heart all those years ago. Making room for new emotions. Making way for life. Really? Could he let go of the anguish that had kept him in limbo for so long and find happiness again?

Was he prepared to take the risk?

Was he prepared not to?

The answers weren't bombarding him, but he could go with the flow for now.

Standing in Kelli's arms, waiting, enjoying a newfound peace within himself as he soaked up the moments drifting by, allowing it to fill him with a relaxing quietness. Across the beach the tide rolled in, reaching up the sand, an occasional gull squawked, and behind them laughter and voices stabbed the air intermittently.

Kelli's lips were moving on his neck, soft yet fiery, gentle yet demanding. Warmth was turning to heat, hot strobes searing him inside and out, building a desire he had to do something about.

His mouth caught hers, his lips demanded possession and his tongue made a foray into her heat. He wanted to lose himself in Kelli, to give as much as he needed to take. His hands cupped her butt, pressed her hard against his need.

'Mac,' she whispered.

His name hung on the night air, vibrating with Kelli's longing. For him. An endorsement of his emotions, of the need to satisfy her too. He scooped her up into his arms and strode fast towards the trees at the end of the bay, which were closer than their room, and way more romantic.

Kelli suddenly started laughing, causing Mac to pause and ask, 'You okay?'

'What is it about us and weddings?'

Phew. 'I have no idea but I'm liking it. We'll have to attend more.'

Her laughter faded. 'Think I've done my dash with those.'

Hey, they might be temporarily engaged but there'd never been any suggestion of a wedding. Mac lowered her to the ground. It was one thing to be rushing to the trees with Kelli in his arms, quite another to stand here holding her discussing unlikely events. Events that came with a dose of reality. This was a temporary situation. 'Let's finish this one before thinking about any more.'

Running her hands down the front of her dress, Kelli had no idea how she affected him. He had to turn away, stare out to sea. Or...

Mac turned back to Kelli, placed his hands on her shoulders and leaned in to kiss her. 'You okay?'

She stared at him for a long moment. 'Yes. Yes, I am.'

Did she just add 'for now' under her breath?

Mac wasn't sure if he wanted to know. If Kelli was hurting then he had to stop all thoughts of sex and kisses. At least until she was comfortable with him again. 'Let's walk a bit more.'

'No, let's kiss, and follow through on that.' She was up on her toes again.

Mac was over talking and trying to analyse everything. Kissing Kelli was way more exciting and rewarding and fun. And kissing was going to lead to those trees.

CHAPTER NINE

'RISE AND SHINE,' Kelli squeaked as the sun inched up over the horizon. 'Let's go kayaking.'

'Didn't you get enough exercise during the night?' Mac groaned as he pulled the pillow over his head.

She tugged it away. 'Nope. I've got energy to burn.'

'Then I know how to fix that.'

Suddenly she was trapped in Mac's arms and sprawled across that big chest. His knee was pushing between her legs, and already she was reacting with need. 'I like your idea.' She grinned before beginning a trail of kisses over his chest, not thinking too much about how she looked this morning.

Or that this was probably her last day as Mac's fiancé. The engagement wouldn't count once back at work.

Nope, she was grabbing everything with both hands and going to have the day of her life with the man she loved. Tomorrow was going to hurt anyway, might as well get as much out of today as possible. And give as much back so as Mac could never say he'd been used, and possibly, just possibly, he might see what he was walking away from and decide not to go. Instead stay and learn to love her.

Kayaking offshore in the morning sun added to the afterglow of their lovemaking and as Kelli powered ahead she couldn't believe the sense of amazement filling her. This was how she'd always imagined being in love would be. But Steve had put paid to that, dampening down any joy she'd felt with him.

Mac paddled up beside her, not slowing, calling as he passed, 'Race you to that boat anchored beyond the bay.' He was off, not waiting to see if she was on for it. He knew she liked a challenge.

He wasn't getting off lightly with this one. She was no stranger to kayaks, having spent many hours in them every summer at the family beach house. She dug deep with the paddle and began a slow, steady overhaul of the kayak in front. Those broad, muscular shoulders could be a distraction—if she let them.

Keeping her eyes fixed on the boat she was aiming for, she managed to keep her hormones in lockdown and begin to draw closer. And closer. Then, 'Hey, slowcoach, stop mucking about and put some elbow into paddling.' Her kayak nosed past, got in front and that was the last she saw of Mac until she reached their target and spun her craft around in the water to gloat. 'And you thought you could beat me.' She grinned moments later as his kayak nudged hers none too softly.

'I didn't want to hurt your feelings,' he gave back.

'Sure, buddy.'

'Not a valid reason for losing? Fair enough. Brunch's on me.'

Everything they ate at the resort was covered by her parents. 'Does that mean we're going into the town? Just the two of us?'

'I'd like to see the town centre.'

'We should check out some of the art shops and galleries. I need a small frame for a photo I got in Fiji.'

'We have a plan. Is it okay we're not joining your family this morning?' Mac looked concerned.

'I bet half them will be in town, doing other things. Today is wind-down time.'

She was right. Seemed every time they turned a corner they'd bump into someone from the wedding party. 'There's no getting away from them,' she muttered.

'Sounding disgruntled, sweetheart,' Mac laughed. 'Did you want time alone with me?'

Sweetheart, eh? Oh, boy. 'Yes, I did.'

His eyes widened before he took her hand and dragged her along to the end of the street and a café overlooking the water. 'In here, quick, before we're spotted.'

As long as no one else had beaten them to the place. 'This is like running from the media,' she quipped.

'You know about that?' Surprise blinked out at her from those stunning green eyes.

She elbowed him. 'I might've been famous in another life.'

'Thought I recognised you from somewhere.' He nodded at a waitress. 'A table for two, please.'

As Kelli slipped onto the chair he held out, she grimaced. 'Too often I saw Tamara trying to avoid the press. It was harrowing when all she wanted was to be left alone to get over what that awful man did by stealing her family's fortune.'

Mac sat beside her. 'She's moved on. There was no looking back at their wedding.'

'You're right. She's so happy in love.' If Tamara had got another crack at the love game surely *she* was entitled to a chance? With Mac? He was her pick. And she was entitled. Just not trusting herself yet.

'What are you having for breakfast? Salad? Or something decadent?' Mac teased.

'After all the exercise I've had? Eggs Benedict at least. Or should that be pancakes with berries and maple syrup?' She licked her lips and tried to ignore the way Mac's gaze fixed on them. 'What are you having?' she asked mischievously.

'What?' His gaze lifted to meet hers, and his eyes filled with lust. Or was that something stronger?

'Eggs for you?' She'd love to give him what he wanted. Again. Making love had never been so incredible, so exquisite, so—everything.

'Stop looking at me with those eyes,' her lover growled.

'They're the only ones I've got.'

Then the waitress interrupted the fun, and they had to make up their minds what they were going to eat. Kelli figured a plate of chaff could be put in front of her and she'd hardly notice, the distraction sitting opposite her large.

Afterwards, out in the sunshine, heading towards an art shop, Kelli felt as if she were walking on air. She was living in a magic bubble, and refused to acknowledge it was about to pop. Not this morning, hopefully not any time today, and that was enough to be getting on with for now.

Mac strode along beside Kelli, his hands firmly jammed in his pockets. The morning was turning into one of the best he'd had in a long time. *The* best. Which was why he had to hold back and not grab Kelli's hand in his and swing their arms between them while feeling her heat zing through his palm and into his veins.

Tipping into the well of excitement and happiness was all too easy to go along with, and would have consequences he wasn't prepared to face. It wasn't as though the pain of losing Cherie would suddenly disappear in a flash of lust. No, the pain was a familiar jacket he'd worn day and night since Cherie left him. Strange how comfortable that jacket was. Safety. Safety from the fear of trying again, moving forward. He'd had the love of his life. No one got two shots at that.

Billy has.

Mac stumbled. Where was he going with this? His eyes sought out Kelli, drank her in. His heart curled in on itself, tightened that comfort jacket around him. Kelli needed someone to love her with no restraint, and he couldn't guarantee that.

'Hey, Billy, Leanne, didn't expect to see you two out of your rooms before midday.' Kelli rushed to her brother to wrap him in a hug before giving Leanne one.

Had his thoughts conjured up Billy? The man looked relaxed and utterly happy. So it was possible to start again. Mac gave Leanne a light hug and Billy a back slap. 'Great wedding, guys.'

Billy, the man who'd faced tragedy and moved on to find new happiness, grinned. 'We thought so.'

Did he ever worry about losing Leanne? About history repeating itself? He had to. He was human. 'I was glad to be a part of the proceedings.'

'The family will be gearing up for another wedding now ours is done and dusted.' Billy smiled. 'Any idea when you might tie the knot, sis?'

Kelli's face paled. 'Um…no, not yet. There's plenty of time, no need to rush.'

Mac moved closer to her, said, 'We'll make some decisions later.'

'Watching you two together, I'd have said next week would be a good time.' Leanne fanned her face with her hand. 'I mean, you two are hot together.'

Draping an arm over Kelli's shoulders, Mac struggled to come up with something to deflect these two who only meant the best for Kelli. 'We'll keep you posted. Now we need to get to the art shop, and I presume you've got lots you want to do before heading to the airport for your flight to Australia.'

'Have a great honeymoon, you two.' Kelli put her arm around his waist and began to walk away. 'Spare me all the details when you get back.' Laughter followed them down the road. 'Phew,' she muttered.

'It's getting harder, isn't it?'

Her shoulders rose and fell under his arm. 'It sure is.'

One day to get through and then Kelli would release him from their engagement, mission accomplished. 'Jason's been great about the whole thing.'

Kelli slipped out from under his arm. 'He's been brilliant.'

'I wonder if he'd felt obligated to your parents for everything they've done for him?'

Kelli's eyes all but popped out of her head. 'He'd go so far as to marry me because of that?'

'You work it out. You know him and your family better than I do.' The more Mac thought about it, the more he felt he'd hit the button bang on. 'It's not too late to set the record straight.'

The nibbling stopped. 'Because when everyone learns you and I are not engaged the pressure's going back on? Got you. I'll talk to Jason later.'

'Good. Now let's enjoy what's left of our time together.' He pointed to a shop. 'Is that where we're headed?'

With a nod Kelli changed direction, aiming for the wide store with big windows letting in lots of sunlight. Inside paintings dotted the walls, placed artfully so as not to encroach on the next and spoil the viewer's enjoyment of what was on the canvas.

Kelli wandered around the room, stopping to gaze at

two paintings in particular. 'If only I had a big house to put works of art like these in.' She sighed wistfully as she studied a watercolour of Rangitoto Island with a storm brewing around the peak. 'That is particularly beautiful. Brings back memories of a day when Dad took me and Phil across to walk to the top. We got soaked, but I didn't care. It was wonderful being on the island with only a couple of other people also walking the track to the summit.'

'You wouldn't want it where you live now?' Mac asked.

'It would have to go in my bedroom and that's small and dark. No, that painting needs light and space to itself.' She moved on.

What if he bought it for her? As a gift for a wonderful weekend? No. Not wise. She might misinterpret the gesture, think he wanted more from her, or think he was trying to buy his way into her bed again. Moving along, he studied the next two paintings, liked them but wasn't overly moved. But the next one brought him up short. An abstract that spoke to him of tension and danger and risks and a softening in one corner that said maybe good things could happen if he was prepared to open up to them.

Mac stared and stared, taking in the brush strokes almost one by one. Dazzling red shades, subtle greens, angry blues, and a hint of summer blue. The more he looked, the more he found. He didn't do art, wasn't into paintings and pictures at all.

Kelli nudged him. 'Buy it.'

'No.' Apart from a calendar and a photo of Mum with him and Cherie his apartment walls were bare. Sterile. Safe. Undemanding.

'Dare you.' The challenge was loud and clear.

He wasn't having a bar of it. Not this one. He shook his head abruptly. 'You finished in here?'

'Sure.' She followed quietly, but he could feel her eyes boring into the back of his skull.

Out on the footpath he looked around, saw a pottery shop and headed that way. 'Let's look in there.'

'Okay,' was all she said, but her disappointment was obvious. She expected more of him. An explanation for starters.

'You're not keen on pottery?' he asked.

'Not my thing. Whereas paintings are. Especially when it grabs me and won't let me walk away. Then I know it's special. Like that one did for you.' She changed direction, heading for the beach.

Why did Kelli think one painting mattered? It wasn't as though he'd shouted with glee or said he had to have it. No, he'd studied it in depth, that was all. Then he'd walked away, leaving it behind where it couldn't bug him every time he saw it.

'Where do you live?' Kelli asked out of left field. Or maybe it wasn't given he'd been looking at a painting and decided not to buy it.

'In a Ponsonby apartment.' It was modern, comfortable and boring. That painting would liven the place up no end.

'Yours? Or do you rent?'

'It's mine.'

'Any flatmates?'

'No.'

'Pets?' she persisted.

What was this? Fifty questions? Might be lucky if she stopped at fifty. 'I occasionally toss the neighbour's spaniel a bone. Does that count?'

Kelli was shaking her head over something he didn't get. 'Sounds lonely. I bet your walls are bare and the furniture is minimal.'

'It's perfect.'

'Speaks of lack of involvement.'

He'd done that deliberately. 'Okay, I'll play ball with pooch next time I see him.'

'Stop being a prat, Mac.' Anger glittered out of those serious eyes, directed solely at him. 'Why did you come here with me if you don't want to mix with people?'

Go for the solar plexus, why don't you?

'I told you. You needed help and I offered.'

Her hands were on her hips, her feet slightly splayed. 'So you said, but I don't buy it. You've fitted right in. You are a people person, Mac. Don't say you don't like most of them back.'

'I used to be a people person.' But Kelli had a valid point. 'You're right. I've enjoyed myself immensely these past couple of days. I've remembered what it's like to be involved with friends, and to have someone special at my side.' Ouch. Shouldn't have said that. 'That special person is you, Kelli. I have no idea where we're going with what started out as a solution to your problem, but I do like you a lot.' Like? Pathetic. But as far as he was prepared to go for now. The most he'd admit even to himself.

'Thank you, I think.' She wasn't smiling at him, or bursting with happiness.

Did Kelli expect more of him? Slam. What if she didn't like him half as much as he did her? He'd set himself up for a crash. He'd better toughen up and get over himself. This was what getting involved meant. Suddenly he thought he might want more with Kelli, that he mightn't be happy to rock off into the sunset come Monday. Was this love? He did not know. It didn't feel like last time. Could be it was taking the long way round to his heart. If it wasn't then it could be the beginning of a strong friendship. Mac shuddered. Being friends with Kelli was imperative, but nowhere near enough.

Kelli leaned close and placed the softest of kisses on his mouth, then she took his hand. 'We're going back to the art shop and you are going to buy yourself a painting. It's past time you got out in the real world again.'

'And you think a painting is the answer?'

She stopped at that, turned so her fierce cobalt gaze locked on him. 'You felt that painting—the moods it invoked were there in your eyes, on your face. It pulled you right in and touched something deep. I don't know what that was but I do know that painting has your name on it.'

'What if I don't want to look at it every day and feel those emotions it brought back?'

She hesitated, and he thought he'd won. But no, this was Kelli. 'Maybe it's time you did feel all those emotions you've obviously kept clamped down deep inside. Maybe you're ready to face living fully again, moving on and finding happiness. Everyone deserves it, Mac. Even you.'

Blimey, she didn't hold back. Gave it like a metal truck dumping its load at the quarry. It was too much to take in right now. He did best when he let thoughts and emotions infiltrate slowly, one fact at a time. 'What about you? Don't you deserve it too?'

'I wasn't aware I was avoiding it,' was her acerbic retort.

'Oh, really?'

'I am not shutting out happiness. I'm just afraid I won't find anyone to love me enough to overlook my imperfections so that I can trust that happiness.'

Her ex had done a right number on her. What he wouldn't like to do to him. How to put his feelings out there without getting too involved and giving Kelli hope he was afraid to follow up on? 'I truly don't understand. You are so beautiful, inside and out. No one's perfect but in my book you're damned close.'

Her mouth fell open, quickly followed by tears tracking down her cheeks. He wrapped her into a tight hug, his shirt getting a soaking and his heart a pounding.

When Kelli finally pulled back in his arms to look at him, she asked, 'What are we doing to each other?'

Setting ourselves up for a big fall. 'Telling it how we see it. Being honest, in other words.' Except he wasn't totally. Opening his heart wasn't— A scream shattered the fragile air around them. 'What's going on?' Mac stared around the shops and the street, saw two women running out of a café, and headed their way.

'The chef's been electrocuted!' one of them shouted. 'We need help. I think his heart's stopped.'

Help. Mac's key word. 'I'm a doctor. Kelli here's a nurse.' He looked around at the shocked faces of pedestrians. 'Is anyone a local? We need to find a defibrillator.'

'There's one in the superette. I'll grab it,' a man called, already racing away.

Kelli ran into the café, pushing through the throng of people gaping into the interior, not waiting for anything.

Mac took after her. Arriving in the kitchen, he heard Kelli ask as she knelt beside the stricken young chef, 'How long has she been down?'

'A minute, a bit longer.' The guy swallowed. 'Lauren— she was using the hand-beater, whipping the gravy. It must've short-circuited.' Another swallow. 'I'm the manager, haven't had anything like this happen before.'

'Stay clear everyone,' Mac warned. 'Don't touch that beater,' he snapped at Kelli as she reached for the girl's hand gripping the utensil.

'I've turned off the power to the switches,' the manager informed them.

Kelli was onto it, immediately kicking the beater out

of Lauren's hand, then starting CPR. The girl was pale as sand while blue around her lips.

'Where's that defib?' Mac asked as he dropped to his knees on the other side of their patient. 'Have you called the ambulance?' He flicked a quick look to the manager.

'They're on their way.' The man was calming down now that he had medical help for his chef. 'So's the air ambulance.'

'Here's the defib,' someone yelled.

'Get it charging,' Mac instructed as he tore Lauren's chef jacket down the middle. 'Wish we had some oxygen.'

Kelli kept up the compressions, a sweat breaking out on her forehead. 'Your wish is about to be granted. I hear a siren.'

'Clear the area around your patient,' intoned the defibrillator.

'Everyone stand back,' Mac repeated the message as he placed the paddles on Lauren's chest. With a quick glance around to make sure those in the room had heeded his request, he shocked the chef.

Her body jerked upward, fell back.

Feeling for a pulse, Kelli shook her head.

'Stand back,' Mac commanded though no one had moved.

Another shock, another jerk off the floor, and then a flicker of an eyelid, a slight rise of Lauren's chest.

'Yay, we have a result.' Kelli huffed air over her lips. 'A good result.' Her fingers were on the pulse, nodding as she silently counted the beats.

'The best.' Mac sat back on his haunches as paramedics rushed purposefully into the room, carrying oxygen and all the other necessary paraphernalia to keep Lauren alive and well. Quickly explaining what he knew, he moved out of the way and left the experts to the job.

'That calls for a very strong coffee,' he told Kelli as they walked through the humming café.

The talking stopped and clapping broke out.

The manager pointed to a table out on the pavement. 'Take a seat and I'll bring you those coffees. On the house. I can't thank you enough for your rapid response. Lauren was very lucky you were in town.'

'Glad to be of help,' Mac agreed.

'How do you take your coffees?'

With their orders in place Mac settled on a seat and stretched his legs along the side of the table. 'Things like what just happened remind me why I became a doctor. The unexpected can happen to anyone anywhere and it's an awesome feeling being able to step in and do something constructive.' He was feeling good.

'Then you should shout yourself a reward. That painting's got your name on it.' Kelli grinned at him. Then her breath seemed to hitch in her throat and her teeth did that nibbly thing on her bottom lip as the grin faded. She looked away as her cheeks began turning a strawberry shade.

Mac understood that breathing problem. It was going on in his lungs too. He didn't think his cheeks had taken on the red hue but he definitely wanted to nibble something. His brain was not in sync with the rest of his body. 'We don't have to wait for the coffee.'

'Here you go, folks.' Two large cups appeared on the periphery of Mac's vision, along with a plate of chocolate and strawberry muffins. Strawberry? Yes, the same shade as Kelli's cheeks. 'Thanks,' he muttered.

'Thank you,' Kelli told the hovering manager and picked up the huge coffee cup and wrapped her shaking hands around it. 'Those muffins look delicious.'

Don't spill the coffee, Mac warned silently. *We'll be*

here all day while another round is made and more food brought out.

She must've got the message because her grip tightened.

'You're welcome.' Finally the guy moved off.

'Isn't that too hot to hold onto?' Mac queried lamely, all out of what to say to her without double entendre. Her fingers had to be burning.

The colour in Kelli's cheeks intensified. She sipped at the frothy milk on top of her coffee. Still not looking at him.

Now what? Hot? Too hot to hold onto? She had it bad. So did he. His gut had tightened in anticipation. 'I suppose it would be rude to leave right now,' he half asked, half stated.

Kelli nodded emphatically, making a moue with her mouth. 'I reckon.'

'And this *is* too hot.' He blew on his long black. 'Boiling, can't drink it just yet.'

Suddenly Kelli laughed, a free and happy sound that went straight to his heart. 'I hope the resort staff haven't cleaned our room and sent our bags to the luggage room yet.'

Mac wanted to wrap her hand in his, kiss her knuckles, knew that'd only turn him on even more. 'We don't have to be out until two. Should be just enough time for what's on your mind.'

Those alluring eyes widened, and colour crept into her cheeks again. 'My mind hasn't a lot to say at the moment. Except we are going back to that art shop on the way to the resort.'

'Persistent, aren't you?'

'Yes.'

And he'd better not forget that. Nor could he deny any

longer that he wanted to take another look at the painting. It would look perfect on the west wall of his sitting room, the first thing someone would see when they entered the room. It would demand attention, more than the view of the harbour bridge and the sea beyond. But still he said, 'I don't need a blasted painting any more than I need a pet dog.'

'Don't tempt me.'

CHAPTER TEN

MONDAY, AND KELLI hit the gym before starting work. Her body was exhausted, every muscle had its own tune of cramps and tiredness, but there'd been a lot of serious eating and drinking over the weekend that needed dealing with.

She'd done some weights and was clocking onto the treadmill when that sexy deep voice that lifted bumps on her skin and kept her awake the night before interrupted her concentration.

'Hey, Kelli. Didn't expect to see you in here this early.' Mac strolled into sight.

'I was at a loose end.' Restless and wound up tighter than a ball of string and unable to focus on anything. 'You're early too.'

'I'd done my laundry, cleaned the bathroom and got in groceries for the week, and still had time to kill before going into work.' How Mac managed to step onto the treadmill beside her without doing a face plant was beyond her. He hadn't taken his eyes off her legs from the moment he'd turned up.

Heat and need spread through her, blanketing her hang-ups about her body with something far more exciting and game changing because now she understood what that look meant, had experienced how Mac followed up with his hands and mouth. They were in the middle of the gym, surrounded by people working out. Get real. This was not the place to be craving Mac's touch. Struggling for normality—her old normality—Kelli dredged up an inane comment. 'I did pretty much the same things this morning.'

Mac nodded, still focused on her legs. 'Way too wired to be hanging out doing nothing.'

So he felt the same as she did. There was no holding in the smile now spreading across her face. 'I didn't know you could be so domestic.'

'Needs must,' he grunted as he hit the buttons, finally dragging his eyes forward. 'Now for a hard workout.'

Kelli was already jogging slowly, warming up before hitting the hills button. 'That painting look good on your wall?'

'Yeah.'

'What's wrong? You regretting your purchase?'

'Too late for that. I'm enamoured with it, which is un-nerving. I live a very clean-cut style; no mementos other than one photo, no pictures cluttering the walls, or un-necessary lampshades and furniture to dust.'

Sterile. Uninvolved. 'Keeping the world at arm's length.' He'd have fifty fits if he saw her bedroom.

'It's who I am, Kelli.' Oh-oh, the serious tone had switched on. 'You'd best remember that.'

Her stomach knotted. 'Hard to gel that version of you with the man I spent the weekend with. Sure you like liv-ing so remotely?'

'It's safer that way.'

'Safe can be restrictive,' Kelli argued, knowing she was guilty of doing the same until Mac came into her life.

'Less confronting.'

'To what?' Her heart had already taken a tumble and

there was quite likely a load of pain waiting in the background for the day Mac didn't want to stare at her legs.

A pager sounded and it wasn't until she saw Mac tug something from his waistband that she realised where the peeps had come from.

'There goes my workout.' Mac hit the slow button. 'I'm wanted in ED. Seems Michael's got a problem.'

Kelli nodded, swallowed the flare of annoyance that she'd been relegated to second. As head of department he had to go. It was bad timing, was all. They were actually talking about something serious and probably important to their future. If there was going to be a future, and she had no idea where they stood on that. No point trying to keep Mac here when he was wanted in the department. That was a no go. 'See you later.'

'Back to reality.' A brief twisted smile accompanied his words.

'Saved by the pager,' she acknowledged.

Mac didn't hear her. Or chose not to, striding out of the gym without finishing that uncomfortable conversation.

Suddenly the leftover fizz from the weekend dropped away, leaving her lethargic and barely able to put one foot in front of the other. The bubble had burst. Mac hadn't changed anything. His offer to stand by her had been for the duration of the wedding. No need to discuss breaking up. Confronting her family to explain had always been part of the deal.

The problem was that she'd gone and given away her heart to Mac. Of course she shouldn't have, but that suggested she'd had control over it. Fat chance. Spending so much time with Mac, having fun and getting to know him better, seeing a different side to the serious specialist—what was there not to fall in love with? The sparks had flown, back and forth. Leanne had commented about how hot she and Mac were together and that took involvement from both parties.

Involvement, Mac. When you get close to someone. When you share things—conversations, meals, friends and family. Involvement.

Sweat trickled down her back, soaked the waistband of her knee-length sports pants. *Yuck.* Her legs protested every step and her lungs moved in and out as if they were under water. Was she drowning? Under a blanket of unrequited love? Whatever Mac thought was a mystery. She'd seen desire light up his eyes uncountable times over the past three days. Had been loved with skill and abandonment, with wonder and joy. *What do you think of me, Mac? Huh? Do you care enough to carry on seeing me?*

Her legs won. No point in hauling them through the kilometres when they moved like lead weights.

Hitting the 'stop' button, she lurched against the hand bar and kept her balance. Just. Time for a shower and a coffee then she'd sign on for the shift.

Hopefully Mac would be friendly and not doing his serious thing as if she was a problem that had to be put in its box.

The department was full to bursting when Kelli slouched in. Mac was nowhere to be seen for handover, and those in the day shift were subdued. Too quiet.

'What's going on?' Kelli asked Stephanie, who'd been standing behind the counter flicking through patient notes.

'Everyone will hear soon enough.' Then Stephanie sniffed. 'Michael lost a patient, and he's not coping very well. A wee boy with a massive allergic reaction to some food product.'

A wee boy. That was hard to take and, for the doctor

in charge, distressing beyond imagination. 'That's why Mac got that message.' And she'd been thinking he'd been in a hurry to leave her. Selfish didn't begin to cover her thoughts. *Sorry, Mac. Sorry, Michael.*

'They're shut in his office going over what happened. Hopefully Mac can reassure Michael that he did everything right.' Stephanie looked worried.

'That explains the full cubicles. Down a doctor. What was Michael doing on day shift anyway?'

'He started early to cover another registrar who went off sick. One of those kind of days.' Stephanie handed her a file. 'Cubicle three, male, fifty-five, arrhythmia, SOBOE, no known history. Monitor him and I'll send a doctor as soon as I have one available. We need to get things moving around here, even if we only clear some of the minor cases until Mac's able to join us.'

'No problem.' Heading across to the cubicle opposite the department centre where more serious patients were kept under watch, Kelli glanced down the page of notes she'd been handed, took in the relevant details, and tried not to think about Michael and how he must be feeling. The guy was good, didn't make mistakes, but all doctors met their challenges, and today was his turn. 'Hi, Will. I'm Kelli, the nurse who's going to be keeping an eye on you for the next hour or two.'

'A lot of fuss about nothing, if you ask me. You've got far more serious patients needing your attention,' Will blustered.

The woman beside him introduced herself as his wife and said, 'Will, no one's asking you. The nurses are telling you there's something wrong with your heart and if you think I want you at home before we know what's going on, then think again.'

Kelli raised a thumb in the woman's direction. 'Will,

your wife's right. We can't be discharging you only to have you brought back in a far worse condition later, now can we?'

Will blanched. 'I guess not.'

'You've had a shock, physically and mentally.' She was reading the heart monitor's printout. 'See how those peaks are not nice and even? That's an abnormal rhythm and the doctors will want to find out the cause.'

'Am I going to have heart surgery?' All the bluster had gone out of her patient's voice. 'I've never been under the knife before.'

His wife gripped his hand. 'It won't be as serious as that.' The look that she threw Kelli was imploring her to reassure her husband.

'Let's not get ahead of ourselves. Your BP is high, but your lungs are clear of fluid, which is good. I'm here to keep monitoring you. A doctor will be along soon—' cross her fingers '—to explain what's happened and what your treatment might be. He'll discuss your symptoms and results with a cardiologist who will decide the next move.'

Stephanie joined them. 'Because of what's happening elsewhere, I've talked to Penny and she asked that we take blood for a troponin.' Penny being a cardiologist. 'Can you do that, Kelli?'

'Sure can.'

'What's a troponin?' Will asked.

'It's a test to see if you've had a heart attack in the last twenty-four hours. I'd say the cardiologist asked for it because of your problems breathing yesterday when you were trying to walk that hill.' The notes said he'd been on a walking challenge in Cornwall Park and had been stopping every hundred metres or so to get his breath back.

'Told you we should've come in straight away.' His wife looked ready to burst into tears.

Kelli nodded. 'It's okay, you're here now. But—' she aimed for stern '—any time this happens, or any chest pain, you must call an ambulance.'

'I don't like being a bother. It's not like it was urgent.'

'It could've been. We'd prefer to send you home healthy and with no heart problems, than have to deal with the consequences of a heart attack.' Or worse, but the embarrassed look on his face said he'd got the message and didn't need more horrific details. 'Right, I'll get the phlebotomy kit and take that blood sample. The sooner I do that, the sooner we'll know what's going on.'

The blood was taken and sent up to the lab. Kelli regularly checked the monitor printout and reassured her patient nothing had changed for the worse.

She worked with a young woman suffering acute abdo pain in the next cubicle as well. Another registrar had joined the shift and between them they arranged bloods for a CBC and CRP. Appendicitis was on the cards, soon confirmed with an increased white cell count and a raised CRP. The girl disappeared with an orderly, heading to Theatre.

Nearly an hour after she'd come into the department Mac strode into Will's cubicle, his serious face on and his eyes sad. 'Hello, I'm Mac Turner, an emergency doctor,' he said. 'I've read all your results and talked to the cardiologist. The good news is that you haven't had a heart attack.'

'And the bad?' Will asked.

'There's still your irregular heartbeat to sort out. I'm going to put you on blood thinners, starting today, to negate the chances of having a stroke until you see the cardiologist in approximately six weeks when the thinners have had time to stabilise.'

Mac was in efficiency mode, checking off points as

though he held a bulletin board. Kelli watched closely. Saw the distress in the back of his eyes and knew he was worried for Michael. 'You're discharging Will now?'

'Yes. There's nothing untoward going on.' He nodded at their patient. 'You'll have regular INR blood tests to monitor how the thinners are working. I'm emailing a copy of everything to your GP and you should visit her tomorrow to establish what's happening over the next few weeks. Any questions?'

The couple was quiet. Most likely shocked, as was Kelli at Mac's abrupt comments. Unlike him even at his most serious. She could forgive him, knowing he had problems to deal with, but his patient would've expected more.

'Okay, Will, let's take this slowly,' Kelli said as Mac disappeared out of the cubicle. 'No leaping out of bed and dancing around the ward.'

'Am I going to have to sit in a chair all day until I see the specialist?'

'Not at all.' She laughed. 'I was exaggerating just a little. Carry on as normal. But I'm sure you're going to have a hundred questions by nightfall so write them down so you can ask your GP tomorrow.'

Soon he was up and dressed. 'I'll be fine,' he muttered.

'Yes, you will,' Kelli agreed. 'I don't want to see you in here again. In the nicest possible way.'

Mac stood up from the desk when she crossed to pick up a file. 'Thanks. You were great with Will and his wife.'

Only doing what she was trained for. 'What about you? And Michael?'

'Want a quick break? I could do with a coffee.'

And someone to talk to. It hung between them, warming her to her toes. Mac Taylor had turned to her when in need. She glanced around, looking for Stephanie, who was only a couple of metres away at the chute for sending samples to the lab.

Stephanie nodded. 'I've got you covered.'

With a full department she was being extra kind, but then that was Stephanie to a T. 'Won't be long,' Kelli promised as she walked past the senior nurse, hoping she could keep that assurance.

They made instant coffee and took it to Mac's office. 'How's Michael?' Kelli asked the moment the door was shut.

'Badly shaken, and in need of a few hours away from here.'

'Shaken's not too bad, is it?'

Mac's lips twitched. 'No, Kelli, it's not.' Then he got serious again. 'Losing any patient is dreadful, but a child dying is every doctor's worst nightmare.'

She nodded. 'Especially when it's your first in charge of the case.'

'Yeah.' Sadness filled the air. 'My first one was a girl, seven and the cutest little minx you'd ever come across. Meningitis. The family had been hiking in the Rimataka Ranges and by the time they realised Juliette was seriously ill and tried to get her out they were already too late.'

He'd not forgotten her name. 'Yet you still blame yourself.' It was a no brainer. She'd seen it often enough throughout her career.

Mac's mouth turned down and his focus appeared to be miles away. 'It's what we train for, saving people in every eventuality even when we understand that's impossible.'

'Will Michael be all right?'

'He has to be, or take a change in direction as far as his career is concerned. If that sounds harsh, I'm only stating the facts as dealt to me over Juliette. Blunt but true. Unfortunately.' Mac dragged his hands down his face. 'But

I'm thinking Michael will come through this just fine. He's talked about it with me and is going to call me any time it gets on top of him.'

'Talking's good.' Often not a guy thing. Nor hers. Telling all and sundry about the bullies who'd shaped her had never been possible, because that'd be exposing her weaknesses and showing others how to get to her. Of course she'd told Steve. They were in love. But he'd used it against her, saying the bullies had a point and shouldn't she take the opportunity to have surgery. Drinking her bland and now cool coffee, Kelli shuddered. 'Yuk.'

Mac's smile was small but it was coming out, slowly, lightening the atmosphere. 'Not up to Waiheke café standards.'

That coffee at the café where they'd helped the chef had been hot and intense and full of flavour. Not that she'd been thinking of the coffee they'd tried to drink super quick, and the muffins she couldn't taste for all the need in her mouth. Nothing but returning to their suite at the resort had mattered. 'Not a patch,' she replied around the longing building in her again.

Inappropriate, Kells. Mac's worrying for Michael, and recalling his own unhappy medical stories and you're thinking of sex.

Mac did that to her. Stole all sense, replaced it with sex-crazed thoughts—no, make that sensations. Because there was no thinking straight whenever Mac was close, unless they were beside a patient, but that didn't count. He'd tossed her world sideways, leaving her not knowing whether she was up or down, left or right. She was lost. And in love.

'We'd better be getting back to work.' Mac stood up slowly, reluctantly. Even sad he was good enough to want to eat.

Or hug. To give warmth to, to show she understood and cared. Easy. Wrapping her arms around him, she held him tight. 'It's what you do. Help everyone who needs you.'

'I do. It's ingrained in me, and probably Michael feels the same, so when the outcome goes wrong it's hard to accept we're not gods.' The pain in his voice smudged out any arrogance there might've been in that statement.

He was a hero in her book. 'Want to share bacon and eggs at the All-Nighter after work? We can talk some more if you need to vent.'

Or we can hurry through our meals and head to your apartment.

She'd love to see where he'd hung that painting. *Ha.* Right. Sure. On the way to his bedroom maybe. Or on the way out after an intense night. Like going to his place would happen.

Mac's mouth covered hers, not softly but hungrily, taking from her, devouring in his intensity. A kiss like no other. A kiss that said he needed her in a way he hadn't admitted before. A personal way.

Her knees were jelly, tipping her into Mac's long, hard body. Exquisite sensations pummelled her from curled-up toes to skin-tightening forehead. 'Mac,' she groaned between their mouths before immediately pressing her lips back on his. How had she survived before Mac? How could she have believed she knew all about sex, or lovemaking, or whatever it was called. There was no one word to describe what was ripping through her right this moment.

Those lips she hankered after when they weren't available were torn away from hers. 'Work.' Mac's chest was rising and falling rapidly.

Kelli spread her hand flat on his pecs, absorbed his heat and harsh breathing. 'Yeah.'

'Rain check?'

'End of shift.'

Mac smiled a long, slow, knowing smile that went no-where towards toughening up her knees. 'Bacon and eggs at my place.'

Truly? She was being invited into his sanctum? A place no one seemed to be invited to. Sex, food and a glimpse at how Mac lived. This was right up there with being awe-some. 'You're on.'

The light in his eyes dimmed. Just realised what he'd got himself into?

Not about to give him a chance to change his mind she spun out of his arms and aimed for the door, unsteady on those knees. 'Let's get cracking. The busier we are, the sooner the hours will be gone.'

'We haven't just been busy?' His smile was back, wider, cheekier and, yes, a whole load sexier—if that was possible.

Getting through the shift without climbing the walls with need seemed a remote possibility. Flapping her hands in front of her fiery cheeks, she straightened her back and blew Mac a kiss to be going on with. 'That was merely a warm up.'

Mac followed Kelli out into the department, his gaze locked on those endless legs in baggy scrubs. Whoever designed the shapeless, boring outfits hadn't had a woman like Kelli in mind. She filled the loose folds out in all the right places and turned the ugly scrubs into a fashion state-ment. Her butt rounded out the back and was moving in a tantalising way that made his mouth water and his heart do cartwheels. Not thinking about the tightness in his groin.

End of shift was for ever away. Might have to find an empty storeroom next break. So much for moving on from the weekend and calling it a day. He wanted Kelli more than ever. Hadn't got enough of her yet. Would he ever?

He had to. There was an engagement to call off. Once that happened those protective brothers wouldn't allow him near her. Nor would her mother.

A breath hissed over Mac's lips as Kelli reached the counter and leaned over the top for a file. Those scrubs took on a whole other rounded shape as her butt stretched them tight.

She's mine.

'Looks like we've got an urgent case on the way in.' Kelli waved the file at him. 'Sixteen-year-old male, knocked off his skateboard outside school. Suspected fractured tib and fib.'

'How far away?' Mac dragged his concentration back to where it should be.

The buzzer sounded.

'About now, I'm thinking.' Kelli grinned as she thrust the file at him and immediately headed for the ambulance bay.

How was a bloke supposed to focus on a patient when that involved working with a siren?

Drawing air in right down to his stomach, Mac counted to ten and stared at the file in his hand. The words flickered, came into focus, and the details nudged Kelli aside in his mind. The teen had a history of broken bones from skateboarding. Slow learner or a lad who didn't believe in holding back when it came to putting his body on the line?

The only good point was that time would whizz past and the shift would be over sooner than later. And then the fun could really start.

At five past nine Kelli leaned back in the chair where she'd been entering data on her last patient. 'I'm for a coffee. Anyone else?'

The waiting room was suspiciously quiet. It'd probably fill up at ten forty-five and there'd be no getting
away for hours.

Can't happen.

Her body hadn't stopped thrumming with need since
that sizzling kiss in Mac's office. If they didn't get down
and busy together soon she was going to explode.

'I'll be along in five,' Mac called from the resus directly opposite.

'Want me to order your usual?'

'Please.'

Settled in a corner of the cafeteria, two coffees and a
donut that looked as if it'd been made a week ago in front
of her, Kelli read her emails. Nothing earth-shattering. Tamara was still pregnant and getting antsier by the hour.
Dad wanted to do lunch one day this week.

'You've got a donut,' Mac drawled as he dropped into
the chair opposite her.

'I more than made up for it over the weekend with all
that exercise,' she retorted around a grin as she put the
phone down on the table.

'Kelli.' He drew her name out like warm liquid honey.
'Tonight. You want to stay with me?'

Oh, boy. Did she what? 'As in a sleepover in your apartment?'

He spluttered with laughter. 'Something like that.'

The phone rang. 'I could ignore it, but it's Mum.'

'We know she won't go away. Better see what she
wants.' Mac leaned back and sipped his long black.

'Hi, Mum. Getting back to normal now the wedding's
over?' The moment the words were out Kelli wanted them
back. She just knew what was coming and had no way of
stopping any of it.

Mac reached for her donut and took a big bite.

'Hey.' She snatched at it and got cream squeezed over her hand for her trouble. Mac's eyes locked on her as she began licking her fingers clean.

'I thought we could start planning yours.'

See? 'Mum? What did you say?' The donut tasted like glue.

'That you and Mac should come to dinner one night next weekend, then we can set a date and start the ball rolling for your wedding. What do you think?'

That I'm in deep doo-doo.

'There's no rush, Mum.' She couldn't look at Mac. Didn't want to see the truth blaze out from those sexy eyes she dreamed about every night. The fun would be over as soon as she explained to her family she was no longer engaged. It was going to finish when he heard her tell Mum they wouldn't be coming to dinner this weekend. Or any weekend.

'Maybe not in your eyes, Kelli, but I like to be prepared.'

When Kelli remained mute her mother sighed heavily before continuing.

'At least come for a meal. Your father and I would love to spend more time getting to know Mac better.'

Getting harder.

'I'll talk to Mac and get back to you. Love you, Mum.' *Click.*

Now what? All the fun and the greatest sex ever and falling in love with the man responsible had not gone any way to prevent the fact that she needed to tell her parents the truth.

'The game's up?' Mac leaned forward, his hand reaching for hers. 'It doesn't…' He hesitated, stared at her for so long a wart must've begun growing on her chin, and then he leaned back against his chair again.

Raw pain sliced through her. 'It doesn't what?' she asked in a high-pitched squeak.

He shrugged. 'Nothing.'

The pain opened wider. Nothing? This was nothing? The weekend, the way they fitted together so well, how they were opening up to each other was nothing? He knew what her mother had asked. The knowledge was there, darkening those eyes, crowding out the previous look of fun and laughter. 'Nothing. As in we're done now that it's Monday? When you've just invited me to stay at your apartment tonight?'

'The deal was I was your fiancé for the weekend, Kelli. This was how it was always going to end.'

'In the beginning there'd been the suggestion we'd take a couple of weeks before calling it off so it didn't look so obvious it had been a hoax.' *Except I went and fell in love with you.* 'Wait a minute. That kiss earlier on? That was a break-up kiss? A false kiss for a false break up? You weren't really going to take me to your apartment?'

Now he reached for her hands. She was shaking. And so was Mac. Maybe there was hope after all. She'd got it wrong, hadn't given him a chance to say anything before leaping in the deep end to rabbit on and on at him.

'I kissed you because I couldn't not. You're beautiful, amazing, and I have had a wonderful few days. Could go on having some more, but in the end we have to tell your family the truth no matter what we get up to.'

She gaped at him, trying hard to keep up, and failing.

He hadn't finished. 'Your mother's invitation to dinner is the wake-up call we need. Continuing what we've started would only make it all the harder to pull the plug further down the track.'

Pull the plug? Nice turn of phrase for her heart to hear. 'Why do we have to finish at all?' The words were out before she'd thought about them. Thank goodness she hadn't cried out that she loved him. How humiliating would that be?

Her hands were suddenly bereft of warmth, or anything, as they were dumped. Mac's face was white, his lips flat. 'I am so sorry. I never meant for this to happen.'

And she'd thought she couldn't hurt any deeper. The genuineness of those words cut her to the core. 'Of course. Helping people is what you do. Staying around and getting involved is not.' Vitriol was not pretty, but again her tongue had raced away on her.

'I can't do anything about that. I've been involved, married, about to become a father, and lost it all. I am never going there again. You have to understand.' He was pleading with her.

Damn it, her heart softened a little. Of course he'd been hurt dreadfully when he'd lost his wife. And apparently an unborn baby. But did he have to lock his heart up for ever? She was asking that? She who'd never wanted to risk being hurt again? That she'd fallen in love with Mac had been completely by accident, but she was prepared to allow him in. 'Why not give us a chance?'

He looked her up and down, and shook his head. 'I don't think so.'

That look made her feel stupid, told her she still wasn't any good at reading men. Her chair legs screeched across the floor as she leapt up. She wanted to beg, to lick her hand again to create that need in his eyes, place her heart in front of him. But that was how she used to deal with people, always trying to appease them. Not any more. Mac either wanted her or he didn't, and, anyway, it was there in his sad but steady gaze—she'd be wasting her time and making a goat of herself into the bargain.

'Time I went back to work.' Heading for the lift to

take her down to the department, she concentrated on holding back the hot tears gathering in the corners of her eyes. Crying never got her anywhere, and tonight would be no exception.

CHAPTER ELEVEN

MAC SAT ON his deck, a thick jersey keeping the cold out, and looked out at the bridge and harbour and saw nothing. Nothing except the agony in Kelli's eyes.

But hell, was he feeling. A deep pain he'd hoped to never know again. The loss of something so important it paralysed him. Something he hadn't yet had the guts to acknowledge. Love. For. Kelli.

Not ready. Too fast. Can't get involved.

Tipping his head back, he stared up at the cloudy sky. Not visible in the dark, it would be grey, he knew, like his heart, heavy with rain as he was with unshed tears. Despite not wanting to he'd gone and got himself in love with the most wonderful woman walking the city.

Slow learner. Hadn't he spent the years between Cherie's death and now denying the need to love, to cherish and adore a woman? To have someone to bare his soul with, and have hers back? Hadn't he accepted he'd had his chance and needn't expect a second shot at happiness? He'd believed it was impossible to know love twice.

Afraid to take it, more like.

Not that he was happy right now. Far from it. Falling in love was a foolish mistake. Letting it cut him off at the knees worse. If only he'd walked away last night after they'd returned to the city, told Kelli thanks and to have a great life. There'd been no reason to postpone the ending to their pretend engagement. The sooner the better for everyone really.

The fact he couldn't not kiss Kelli again and follow up with wanting to make love had nothing to do with this sense of slip sliding, into an abyss.

When the helicopter had touched down yesterday he and Kelli had had to go in separate directions. Kelli's mother had invited them back to the family home for a barbecue. He'd declined, knowing how close to the wire that would take him. One lie too many. But Kelli had gone. She'd been torn, but he'd nudged her. She adored her family and he'd thought they might have tonight together, stalling on ending their relationship because he was selfish, wanted it all without giving his heart.

Ha. Showed what he knew about anything. He'd done his bit and now they were back to being colleagues in the department. But he was greedy, had wanted one more day, and he'd got it. In spades.

Leaping up, he charged inside and came to an abrupt halt in front of the blasted painting that also messed with his mind. His hands gripped his hips as he stared at it, felt it. From the sharp strokes of colour he knew that his future hung in the balance. He either leapt without looking any further, or he crawled into a hole and hid away until his head and heart returned to normal. Uninvolved normal. Cold. Lonely. Sad. Gutless.

Who'd brought his smile back after dealing with Michael's grief and his own memories of a similar experience? The first person he'd ever let that close since Cherie, and now he'd gone and shunted her out of his life. There'd be no coming back from that horrid conversation in the cafeteria. He'd hurt Kelli. All because he refused to acknowledge his feelings. Yet now that he had nothing would change. The past still held him captive.

His phone chirped. He'd ignore it, didn't want to talk to anyone tonight. But it was nearly two a.m. so unless it was Kelli—unlikely—then it could be an emergency. Or Michael struggling to cope with his day.

The display showed Conor. The thumping in his heart slowed as he pressed talk. 'Hey, man. How's things?'

'I'm a dad. To the cutest little girl you'll ever meet. She's awesome, dude, seriously awesome. Tamara is a legend…twelve hours' labour and yet she's smiling like there's no end to Christmas.'

When Conor paused to take a breath he cut in. 'Congratulations to you both. That's wonderful news. I'm glad it went well.' He felt a heel, as if he was raining on his friend's parade with his stilted comments. But it was all he could manage. His mate had to recognise the distress in his polite words.

Stop thinking of yourself for once.

Thankfully Conor was on a different planet, and the Irish accent thick with excitement. 'She's tiny, and looks like Tam. Wait, I'll send you a photo. You've got to see this.'

An email arrived. 'Hold on, I'm going to check this out.' Without cutting Conor off? 'Keep yabbering on while I crank up the laptop.'

'Wish you were here, man. We could have a beer or three.' Conor laughed as if that were the funniest thing he'd ever said. 'And afterwards Tam would kill me.'

Clicking on Conor's email and bringing up the photo of Tamara holding the most beautiful baby against her breast, Mac felt his heart splinter. 'Oh, man.' Sniff. 'You weren't exaggerating. She's lovely.'

'Gabriella. That's her name.'

'How soon before you're saying Gaby?' Mac struggled to find a chuckle in the thick of tears clogging his throat. If jealous was the word to describe what was suffocating him right now, then he was jealous. He and Cherie had nearly had this. He and Kelli *could* have this.

'Already have,' replied Conor. 'Got the wicked-witch eyes from you know who.' Not that he sounded as if that was a punishment.

Mac bit down on the jealousy. Wrong time and place, if there ever was a right one. It was his choice to be where he was at in his life, no one else's. 'I'm thrilled for you. I know how determined you were not to have a family and now listen to you. Happier than a toddler on chocolate.'

'I don't intend having the low that usually follows that. The cardiologist thinks Gaby's heart is fine, and as that's all I ask for I'm going to run with it. Relax and enjoy my family. Got to go. Mum's calling from Dublin.'

'Catch you tomorrow. Hugs to Tamara.'

Had Conor heard any of that? In his excitement he'd been quick to cut the call.

Mac wanted to call Kelli, share the good news, go over the details. Hear her sweet voice. She'd have been the first person Tamara would've called; they were that tight.

He pushed his phone aside. Time he went to bed and got some shut-eye.

Still running away.

His mate's fabulous luck added to his own uncertainty. Underscored what was missing from his life. As Mac made his way through the darkened apartment as confident as if he had possum vision, he couldn't shake the sense that everything he wanted was right there, beckoning, waiting for him to take that last step, take the risk, chance his heart with Kelli.

* * *

'She's gorgeous,' Kelli whispered through the tears drenching her face, dripping onto her nightwear tee shirt.

'I know,' giggled Tamara. They were on their second phone conversation in less than an hour. 'Who'd have believed I'd produce a child so beautiful?'

'You'll choke on that pride,' Kelli giggled back. It was good to hear Tam so besotted. If ever there was someone who deserved happiness that was Tamara. Her past had been diabolical and then along came Conor and the stars hadn't stopped shining for her friend since. If only there were more stars to go round, she might get a bite of the pie too.

With Mac? Only with Mac. And since that wasn't about to happen any time this century, then she was plumb out of luck.

'You've got to come over to Sydney and meet Gabriella,' Tam was yabbering on. 'Asap. She'll grow so fast you'll miss so much.'

'I'll flip across for a weekend as soon as I can arrange it.' That'd give her something to focus on rather than an unobtainable man and the heartache he'd started up for her. 'With a bit of luck I'll get flights that fit in with my shifts. I can't ask for another Friday off just yet.'

'Let me know when you've booked.' The giggles had stopped, but the wonder was still in Tam's voice. 'Seriously, Kelli, this motherhood stuff's amazing. I know there are going to be days and nights when I'll be pulling my hair out, but today I fell instantly in love with this little human. She's stolen my heart and I'm never going to let go.'

'Stop it.' Kelli sniffed back another flood. Until now babies had always been on the back burner, something to get serious about later. Couldn't have one without having a partner and she wasn't getting tied to any man to be trashed again. Then along came Mac, cool as, sexy as, kind and fun as. And bang. All the theories in the world sloped out of the back door leaving her slam dunked in love.

'Was Mac as hot as you'd hoped?'

Where did that come from? 'Sure, he's hot.' That was all she was admitting. The first time she'd ever kept something from her bestie, and it didn't sit easy, but Tam wouldn't let it go if she had any clue.

'Hot to look at? Or hot up close and touching?' drilled her *bestie*.

'Does it matter?'

'Conor, you hold Gabriella for a minute. I've got some serious talking to do here.'

Great, she was in for a speech. 'I've got to go, Tam. It's two-thirty in the morning and I should be sleeping. I'll call tomorrow morning.'

'Don't hang up on me, Kells. You answered my call before the first ring finished so you weren't even trying to sleep.'

Kells. Said it all, really. Even though she knew she wasn't going to like whatever was coming her heart swelled for her friend. 'Go on.' Might as well get it over. Sleep would be impossible anyway.

'I saw you and Mac together at my wedding. Sparks were flying between you.'

'You've told me this.' Could be she was getting off with only a warning.

'So? The weekend? Spill.'

'Just as hot.' More so. 'But there's a catch.'

'Isn't there always? You have to make allowances.'

'Mac went as my fiancé. Not true, of course,' Kelli was quick to point out, just in case Tam got some strange ideas in that sharp head of hers. 'It was meant to put Jason firmly out of the picture and on that score we succeeded.'

Laughter was peeling through cyber into her ear. 'You and Mac pretended to be engaged. Wow, that's way more than I suggested, or believed you'd have the guts to undertake.'

'It's not funny.'

'It's hilarious. Hey, Conor, wait till I tell you this.'

'Hanging up now.' But she didn't. Her fingers tightened around the phone, pressing it painfully hard against her ear. 'Tam, I'm in a fix.'

'You've got to explain to your family. Hope Mac's got medical insurance.' Tam was still laughing.

Anger flared. This was not funny.

Suddenly Tamara sobered up. 'Kells, the family will understand, might even be embarrassed that you had to take such drastic measures. Ah, no, cancel that. They'll tear your hide off, wrap you in big Barnett hugs, and shake Mac's hand for helping you out.'

'I'll keep you posted. Tomorrow has to be the big reveal. I can't go on living under this any longer.' Not when Mac had made it plain they weren't going anywhere.

'What's the real issue here? You gone and got too close to Dr Hunk?'

There shouldn't be any tears left in the tank. Seemed she knew Jack nothing. 'Something like that.'

'What are you going to do about it?' Only sympathy now.

'Tie bricks to my feet and jump off the wharf.'

'Yep, I can see that working. Then again, you could try going with this something, spend more time with Mac, get to know him even better, not only in the sack. Find out if he's the guy you want to spend the rest of your life with.'

She already knew the answer to that.

'Kells? I get it. You do, don't you?'

Again she couldn't find the words to explain herself.

'You're afraid. I get that too. Been there, got the man and baby to show for it. And guess what, I'm over the moon with happiness. I want you to have this. I really do.'

'Easy for you to say,' she croaked.

'Nothing about getting to where I am now was easy. But it was worth all the crap that went down.'

'Mac's not interested in me.' Other than between the sheets, and in the shower, behind the trees. Certainly not as a lifelong partner who might get to know what made him tick. 'Please don't share this with Conor. I know he's your nearest and dearest but I did hold that position platonically for years before he turned up.'

'All between you and me.'

'Thanks. I'd better let you go. You've got a daughter to feed or change or hug. Yes, hug her from me, will you? Love you, Tam.' Kelli cut the call and tossed the phone onto the bedside table.

Telling Tam that much about her feelings for Mac was too much. Not that her friend would ever say a word to anyone else but now she'd enunciated it she could no longer pretend she was in control, no longer pretend that she'd be able to shove her love in a dark corner and forget about it, bring it out only on dull days and Billy's wedding anniversaries. Now she had to face up to the fact she loved Mac with a capital L and that it wasn't going anywhere.

Sleep would never happen tonight. Kelli tossed the bedcovers aside, found her thick dressing gown, the soft, warm, comfort blanket one that did nothing to enhance her figure but a lot to soothe her jangled nerves, and went to boot up the laptop. If she couldn't rest then she might as well make use of the time and check out flights to Sydney.

* * *

'Look at these gorgeous pictures of Gabriella, Stephanie.' Kelli handed her phone over to the head nurse. 'Tam had her at midnight Australia time last night. Isn't she a little cutey?'

'Mac showed me a couple of photos earlier. She's gorgeous.' Stephanie sighed. 'Lucky girl.'

'You want babies?' Kelli asked. So Mac hadn't been backward in sharing the news. His usual reticence about friendships must be missing. Where was he anyway? She'd been vigilant when she'd entered the department, not wanting to be caught unawares in case she gave herself away to those all-seeing eyes.

'Sure. Don't you some time?'

'Haven't given it too much thought. Got other things to sort before worrying about getting pregnant, if you know what I mean.'

'Figured you were halfway to getting that done.' Stephanie handed the phone back, a big, cheeky grin on her dial.

'Nope. Haven't even started,' Kelli told her. 'Who have you got for me?' She held out a hand for a patient report form.

'We'll have handover first,' came the steady, uninvolved voice of the man who'd kept her awake all night.

Plastering on a smile as false as her engagement, Kelli slowly turned to face Mac. *'No problemo.'* Not like everything else.

'I called around to your place after lunch but you weren't answering the door,' Mac told her.

'I was out.' His face paled. Tough. 'Shopping.' Nothing like a bit of retail therapy.

'Not having lunch with your parents, then?'

'I look whole, don't I?'

His eyes scanned the length of her, hesitating at her breasts. 'We need to talk about that.'

'There's nothing to talk about. I've got it sorted.'

'You've told them?'

'Not yet. But I will. On my own.'

His nod was abrupt. 'Right.' He glanced around, found they had an audience, and shivered. 'Listen up, everyone. I'm sure you've all heard the news about Conor and Tamara's baby arriving last night. Gabriella. What say we all put in and send flowers to the happy family?'

Amongst murmurings of agreement Kelli watched Mac. Shadows darkened his upper cheeks, filled his eyes. As if he hadn't slept either. It was going to be a long week. If only she'd been able to get a flight across the Tasman for Saturday but there was a rugby league match on between New Zealand and Australia in Sydney and not a seat to spare. She'd even checked business class thinking the money would be worth it if it got her out of town. But that'd been a waste of time. She'd just have to go hiking on Rangitoto Island all weekend, up and down, up and down, ten times till the ferry returned late Sunday to pick her up.

The ambulance bay buzzer buzzed. Loud, demanding, and the perfect solution to wanting to get away from standing in the same air as Mac.

Michael nodded at her. 'You and me. Let's go see what we've got.' So he hadn't been listening to handover either. Hopefully that wasn't an ongoing problem from yesterday and the patient he'd lost.

'Sure.'

They got a hit and run patient. Broken legs, fractured ribs, and a smashed spleen, which kept them busy for a long time, only to be followed by a stroke victim arriving towards the end of his golden hour. The man survived but was a long way from walking and talking as he used to. As an orderly wheeled him away Kelli stretched up onto her toes and rubbed the small of her back. Exhaustion oozed out of every pore. A big weekend, no sleep last night and being constantly on guard around Mac had taken its toll. And there were more than five hours to go.

Looking around, she spied Mac busy in resus one with a patient whose heart had stopped, and must be where the emergency buzzer had come from. 'I'm going for my break,' she told Michael and Stephanie. Without Mac, and any discussion about telling her family what they'd done.

Sinking onto a hard chair in the cafeteria, Kelli stared into the depths of murky coffee and fiddled with the dried arrangement that was supposed to be a sandwich. No appetite for anything—she couldn't even find the energy to lift either hand to her mouth for liquid or food. The room was rolling around her, as if she were sitting in the centre of a merry-go-round watching the horses rising and falling on their poles. Her eyelids were heavier than pot lids and eventually she gave up fighting to keep them open. Her chin tapped her sternum, and still those blasted horses kept bobbing up and down.

Mac strode into the cafeteria, scanning the mostly empty tables until his gaze alighted on the object of his search. No wonder Kelli hadn't returned from her break. She was sound asleep.

After ordering a long black and a cappuccino from the annoyingly perky girl behind the counter, he crossed and sat opposite Kelli. In sleep she looked vulnerable. And beautiful, but then she looked that all the time. Back to the vulnerable. There were definitely some issues from her past that had kept her hands up in the off-limits zone— until last weekend.

But then he'd appreciated that, wanting nothing more

involved than a fling with her, and he hadn't even realised that until he'd spent three days—and two incredible nights—with her.

Or had the slippery slide into getting close to Kelli
begun in Sydney? Yes, buster, it probably had.

Whichever, letting go was proving impossible. So he
had to find out what those issues were. The bullies? The
guy she'd been engaged to before had done a number on
her. Had someone else been as cruel? There weren't any
problems regarding her family. They all got on brilliantly.

But by knowing what could hurt her he could shore
up his resolve to walk away while he still could. Cruel
to be kind. His guilt at not coping when he lost someone
was stronger now that Kelli had become special. Special?
Come on. Admit that this stabbing in his chest had nothing
to do with special and all to do with... With... He could
not say the word. There was a roadblock in the way. A
roadblock in the form of heartache and lost love and feeling more secure when he only had himself to look out for.

Their coffees were on the way. Mac put a finger to his
lips as the girl got closer and smiled his thanks as she
placed the mugs ever so carefully on the table.

Kelli hadn't moved once since he'd joined her, and the
aroma of fresh coffee didn't awaken her. A thick strand of
that glorious hair had fallen across her face and he ached
to lift it away, but daredn't. If she awoke while he was
doing that she'd have fifty fits and go ballistic.

Which was what he should do. Return to the department and pretend he hadn't been here. But Kelli would
look for an explanation for the coffee and the girl behind the counter would be happy to oblige for sure. Anyway Kelli had to return to work soon or the others would
start asking where she was. He could cover for her. Why

wouldn't he? If he cared about her why not do something so small but hopefully kind?

Mac stood up too quickly, causing the chair to scrape on the floor.

Kelli moved. Her eyes blinked before her chin sagged back on her chest.

He'd got away with it. Leaving the chair where it was, he turned away.

'Mac?' When his name was sleep-filled on Kelli's tongue it sounded warm and tender and loving.

He had to look over his shoulder. Had to. His heart did loop the loop at the sight of Kelli leaning back, still blinking away the sleep and staring at him as though she wasn't sure where she was. He told her, 'There's a cappuccino. Get it into you before coming back.'

Her gaze dropped to the table, returned to him. 'You not drinking your coffee now that I'm awake?'

Not so asleep any more. Acerbic and annoyed instead. 'I wasn't running away.' Those lush lips didn't lift anywhere near a glimmer of a smile. 'I just didn't want to wake you.'

'Then have your coffee.' When he didn't move she snapped, 'Get over yourself, Mac. We can be civil enough to share our break.'

'You're right.' Reaching for the chair, he spun it around to straddle the seat. Like a wall between them. There was no getting any of this right. 'You didn't sleep much last night with Tamara phoning and everything?'

'No.' Kelli tested the heat of her coffee with a slow sip, sending his gut into turmoil. When she replaced the mug on the table there was a smudge of frothy milk on her upper lip. He even began to lift his hand to wipe it away, froze. Not wise. Worse, Kelli's tongue lapped her mouth, removing the froth.

Mac's mouth dried. That tongue had done wondrous things on his skin. South of his belt there was a load of tightening going on. 'I'll see you back in the department.' Whether she could understand him when his tongue was stuck to the roof of his mouth was anyone's guess, but he was out of there before he did something they'd both regret. Like rekindle everything that had been between them all weekend, the heat and need that had driven them into that super-king-sized bed again and again.

Silence followed him out of the cafeteria, but cobalt eyes were drilling holes between his shoulder blades. Not a good look for getting through the rest of the shift. And this was only Tuesday. Three more nights before he got a break and could tuck his heart out of sight, away from danger. Though there'd be no hiding out in Wellington for the weekend with his mother and her cronies. She'd cancelled, having booked to go to Melbourne shopping with a friend instead.

Too late on the danger factor. What he was supposed to be doing now was raising barriers to save himself any further anguish, to keep Kelli safe.

Because after the coming weekend there'd be another five shifts to get through, again and again and again. Might have to ask Conor to look out for a job for him in Sydney.

CHAPTER TWELVE

THE WEEK WAS HIDEOUS. Every day Mac struggled with going into work, so he'd gone earlier than normal, hiding away in his office doing paperwork until handover. But once shift started there was no avoiding Kelli and that continuous snub she'd managed to hold onto since Monday night.

He'd hurt her. No getting away from that. He was hurting too. Denying his love for her was a fail. It didn't go away, instead held his heart in a vice, shaking his carefully put-together world like that seven-point-eight earthquake last year in Kaikoura. The damage felt as monumental. Hopefully the repair work wouldn't be as long as some of the roads and railway lines were going to take down south.

He wouldn't survive like this.

I want you, Kelli. In my home, my bed, my life. Everywhere I breathe.

Now it was Friday night. No more mucking around. He had to talk to Kelli, lay his heart on the line and hope like stink she didn't jump all over it.

Over the week Mac had picked up the phone twice to call Billy and ask how he'd allowed himself to be happy again and both times he'd put it away. The guy was on his honeymoon and didn't need some nutter asking difficult questions. He had to work this out for himself or the happiness would be shallow.

But it was the moving-forward bit he was stuck on.

'Goodnight, everyone. Have a great weekend.' Kelli waved a hand over her shoulder as she headed for the stairway leading to the basement, not a glance in his direction.

Right. 'See you all on Monday.' He headed the same way.

She didn't look back when she pushed her way through the heavy doors, just charged down the stairs as if she was late for something.

Mac raced down behind her. 'Hey, Kelli, you heading home or to the gym?'

Kelli kept moving.

'Kelli, wait.' *Please. Okay,* 'Please?'

Her pace slowed but she didn't stop.

As Mac caught up he forced himself not to let those sad eyes put him off his stride. 'Going to the gym?'

'No. Home to a mug of soup and some tea.'

'A woman could get an ulcer on that diet.' Mac put a hand out to stop her mad dash and looked directly into those beautiful eyes. 'Want to hit the All-Nighter for bacon and eggs? Or lash out and try something different?'

'No, thanks.' She pushed past his hand.

He was right beside her, his steps matching hers. The only thing they had in sync at the moment. 'Any chance of a rethink on that?'

She snapped, 'What's the point, Mac? It's over, whatever it was going on between us. You put your hand up for the weekend, and today is Friday, tomorrow heralds a new weekend, one that doesn't involve us doing things together. You're free to do whatever you like as long as it doesn't involve me.' *Ouch.* Go for the throat, why didn't she? Then, 'What happened to going to Wellington for your mother's birthday?'

They'd reached the landing between floor one and the basement. She carried on down. He followed. 'My mother's flown to Aussie with a friend. But before you even think it, that is not why I asked you to join me for a meal. I want to talk with you.'

'I can't imagine there's anything I want to hear.' She glared at him. 'That's still a no from me.'

'Have you told your family yet?'

She understood what he was talking about. 'Tomorrow at dinner.'

Less than twenty-four hours to change her mind. 'Give me a chance. Come and hear me out.'

'I already listened once, didn't like what I heard.' Kelli stopped one stair below and stared up at him as though wondering how she was going to get it across to him. 'You aren't ready for what I want, Mac. Might never be. Best you spend your energy sorting yourself out.' That steady gaze seemed stuck on him. As though she couldn't look away.

He winced. 'You didn't used to be so hard hitting.'

'I've finally learned to protect myself.' Now she turned away. Slowly but oh-so deliberately. 'See you Monday, Mac.' There wasn't a shred of sarcasm in her voice. Just deep sadness.

'Don't do it, Kelli,' he called after her. 'We're right together.'

Her foot missed the next step and she pitched forward.

Mac reached her as she grabbed at the rail to stop from falling. His heart was going crazy as fear of her hurting herself hit him. He grasped her upper arm, held her tight, close to his body, but not so close as to crowd her. 'Kelli. You crazy girl, not looking where you're going.'

'Don't call me crazy.' She was trembling. Which didn't stop her tugging free and stepping away. 'Though it is a new one for me.'

Mac sat down, held her eye. 'Join me.'

If only he knew how to banish that load of caution darkening the cobalt in his favourite eyes.

'So you can go on and on about why we should remain engaged after telling me there was no future for us? No, Mac. I heard your message, loud and clear. I am not setting myself up to be dropped when the use-by date rocks around.'

She hadn't moved away. Good sign? Or wishful thinking on his part? 'I know you've been hurt in the past.'

'Yep. We both have.' Her eyes slowly lowered to stare down the stairwell. 'Goodnight, Mac.' That sounded, felt, like goodbye. He watched her take a step down, and another, another. On the next landing she looked up, her eyes bleak. 'Enjoy your weekend. Get out and do something rash, like go fishing, or play a round of golf. Get involved with people.'

In other words, get a life.

'What do you want, Kelli? A fling? A wedding? The whole nine yards with kids and a home? Or are you serious about calling this quits?' When she said nothing he continued. 'When we started out I got the feeling you weren't willing to take a chance on any of the happy-ever-after stuff. That you believed everyone was out to hurt you one way or another. So come on. Tell me.'

'It doesn't matter any more.'

'Yes, it does, sweetheart. I know this now. I have been an ass, afraid to step outside my comfort zone, scared to give you my heart. I have been hiding behind Cherie's death for so long it was easier to stay there. Do you feel like that?'

Kelli lifted her gaze back onto him. A bleak gaze that had him fighting not to leap up and hold her tight. Do that and they'd be no further ahead. 'Don't turn everything back on me, Mac. You have issues from here to Africa and I don't hear you talking about them.'

Don't give this woman a laser gun. Her aim was phenomenal. 'Cherie's gone. It wasn't her fault she died, any more than I could've saved her had I known what was happening. It's taken you to wake me up from the guilt. Because I want to be with you. I want *us.* She'll always be a part of me, but my future is mine. Yours and mine, Kelli.'

The mixture of sorrow and disbelief that stared out at him angered him. He didn't need sympathy or understanding. No, he just wanted to love and be loved. Simple as. Complex as. Hard to do.

'If only it was that easy.' She sank down to sit on the stairs. 'The weekend was unbelievable. For the first time in a long time I have found someone I can trust not to deliberately hurt me. But you're not really ready for involvement, and I get that. It took me long enough to come around. But we only signed up for the weekend, not for ever.' Sadness rolled off her in waves.

Then suddenly she was on her feet again, heading down to her car.

'Kelli, I want to be there when you tell your family our engagement's off.'

'What? You want to be whipped?'

'I want them to know the truth.'

Kelli felt her mouth dry up as she stared at Mac. Did she even know him? *Really* know him?

I trust him. I love him. What more do I want?

'And what would that be?' she squeaked. 'What's your

truth, Mac?' Why was there a knitting needle attacking her stomach? Stab, stab.

'Kelli.' Sweet heaven. Two large, firm hands, familiar hands, on her shoulders, holding her ever so gently. 'Kelli, sweetheart.' Sex in two words. Say her name like that and the man could have anything.

Dragging her eyes upward, she finally locked onto his steady gaze. 'Mac?'

'I don't want to call our engagement off. I want to make it real.'

'I don't understand.' But she might be beginning to. Her stomach was quivering and her head spun, but her heart was strangely steady as a rock.

'I've been a fool, a slow learner. I tried to hold you away when all the time I wanted to drag you so close you could never leave me. Every day I stare at that painting and see what I'm missing out on. I love you, Kelli Barnett. Simple and as complicated as that.' No doubt in his eyes. Not a drop.

She sank a bit under his hands, her knees not as strong as they were meant to be. 'Y-you love me?' Mac loved her. 'You love me,' she shouted, and then heard her words echo up the stairwell.

'Tell the world, why don't you?' A glimmer of a smile appeared, wound through her. 'Is this your way of saying you might reciprocate my feelings?'

'I do. I love you so much it hurts.' Her fist banged between her breasts. 'In here. This week has been hell watching you, hearing you, remembering how well we fit together.' She took a step up, and another to stand beside him. Reached up on her tiptoes. 'Yes, Mac Taylor, I love you.' Her lips sought his, touched lightly.

Mac's arms wound round her, brought her up against that hard, soft, warm body.

She deepened the kiss, lips pressed to lips, her tongue plunging into his mouth, tasting. Her knees weakened some more, so she was forced to lean further into him.

This was what kissing the man she loved felt like. What being kissed by the man who loved her back was all about.

She couldn't get enough.

Eight days later Mac lifted Kelli's case off the luggage carousel at Sydney's Kingsford Smith Airport and groaned. 'What didn't you leave behind?'

'Last week's laundry and a bag of stale crisps.' Her case was stuffed full with toys and cute little dresses for Gabriella that would take at least a year for her to grow into. Kelli pinched those straining arm muscles and grinned. 'Not going all soft on me?'

'Soft?' he chortled. 'Complaining about the goods already?'

Maybe it was their happiness but they were shooed through Immigration so fast they were outside and climbing into a taxi before they'd caught their breaths.

'Darling Harbour, please,' Mac directed the driver, adding the name of the hotel they'd stayed at for Tamara and Conor's wedding.

Kelli felt a knot of excitement unfurling in her tummy. They were going to unload their bags before heading across the city to see Tamara, Conor, and wee Gabriella. Then tonight—anything could happen. So much to be excited about. Her hand sought Mac's.

His fingers wound around hers, giving her a gentle squeeze. 'Welcome back to our special place.'

Her lips found his, and this kiss was no sweet, soft one but a hungry, love-filled one. Bringing everything together for them. When Kelli thought about it she felt her whole life had been heading for this day, this man. Then

Mac's tongue slid into her mouth and danced across her tongue. And she couldn't think any more.

'Excuse me, but here's your hotel,' the driver interrupted them.

They broke apart with an unspoken promise this kiss and its consequences were not over, merely on hold until they were upstairs in their room.

Upstairs on the top floor, Kelli discovered, when the lift doors slid open to reveal two apartments, one apparently theirs for the weekend. 'Oh, Mac, you've gone overboard, but I won't let you change your mind.' She did a twirl of the massive lounge room before going to check out the bedroom and en-suite. 'Come in here. This bed is ridiculous.' It was the size of a football field. 'I'll never find you in the night.'

Mac stood in the doorway, laughing. 'I'll wear reflective pyjamas.'

'The day you wear any pyjamas I'll know you've gone off me.'

His laughter stopped. 'That's never going to happen.'

'Good answer.' Her smile was filled with love for this man who'd seen behind her barriers to the fears that had dogged her most of her life and still loved her. With her forefinger she beckoned him into the room. That bed was made for using, not staring at. 'Come here.'

'Hate to disappoint but we've got a booking down on Darling Harbour.' He didn't look at all repentant, more like cocky. Or was that pleased with himself?

'We have?' What was going on? He hadn't mentioned anything until now. 'We're not going to meet Gabriella?'

'A man's allowed to surprise his woman occasionally.'

Her tummy sucked in on itself. Stepping up to him, she peered into his eyes, trusting him with everything she had. 'Mac?'

'We will be using that bed, just not yet.' He hooked an arm over her shoulders and turned them to the door leading out to the lift.

Once again the excitement was bubbling. 'Where are we going specifically?'

'Which part of "surprise" don't you understand?' he mock growled before dropping a kiss on a particular hot spot below her ear.

Snuggling closer, she refrained from uttering another word for the next ten minutes as they made their way out of the hotel and down to the pier and along to... 'The restaurant Tamara and Conor were married in. Where our gazes got all fogged up staring at each other,' she gasped.

'We're having brunch. Along with champagne. Thought we should celebrate where it all began.' Mac wasn't smiling now; instead he looked purposeful and serious as he gave his name to the waiter.

There was a lot of activity amongst the waiters and the sound of a cork popping, champagne being poured, chairs pulled out, serviettes shaken open, then the staff disappeared.

As Kelli sank onto the chair Mac held for her she caught his hand over her shoulder. 'You're such a romantic, you know that?'

He came around to face her and picked up both glasses and handed her one. Then he dropped to one knee.

Kelli's heart went into overdrive and she had to pinch herself to see if she was alive and this was real. The glass wobbled in her fingers; cool liquid splashed over the rim.

'Kelli.' Mac reached for her other hand. 'I can't imagine my life without you in it. Will you please marry me and make me the happiest man on the planet?'

'You're proposing.'

'Yes, sweetheart, I am. No way were you getting away without a proper proposal.'

'Like I said, a romantic. And yes, Mac Taylor, I will marry you.'

'And make me happy as I will you.'

'All of that.' Leaning forward, she kissed those accomplished lips. 'I love you.'

Pulling back, Mac removed her glass from its precarious hold and placed both on the table before wrapping her into the biggest, warmest, lovingest hug of her life with a kiss to match.

Sometimes life did deliver on your wishes, Kelli acknowledged silently as she melted further into the man who'd brought her all the happiness she could want. More importantly, she was able to pour her heart into giving Mac all his heart's desires.

Then Mac stood up and put his hand in his pocket, retrieved a tiny jeweller's box and opened it, held it out to her. 'I know I should've got you to choose a ring but when I saw this sapphire I had to have it. It's the same cobalt shade as your eyes when you're laughing.'

Slowly she held a now very shaky hand out to him. Her gaze was fixed on the sapphire set in gold. 'It's beautiful,' she choked. 'You got it so right.' Not that she'd have been able to describe something like this if asked.

As the gold band slid onto her finger she sighed. What a ride, but worth every bump and glitch along the way to be here with Mac.

Sure, there was champagne, and a ring, and Mac had got down on his knees, but this time she heard the love, the genuine need to be with her and love and cherish her and accept her as she was. Love. This proposal was all about love, the right kind of love. Sharing, caring, happy.

Picking up the glasses again, she handed one to Mac

and raised hers. 'To us, and whatever the future brings.'
They had another wedding to look forward to.

Mac clinked his glass against hers. 'To us, my love.'

And then they drank the nectar of love, the bubbles
fizzing along Kelli's veins to her toes, along her fingers
where that ring gleamed, and slap bang into her heart
where her love for Mac sat ready for anything.

* * * * *

*If you enjoyed this story, check out
these other great reads
from Sue MacKay:*

*PREGNANT WITH THE BOSS'S BABY
RESISTING HER ARMY DOC RIVAL
THE ARMY DOC'S BABY BOMBSHELL
DR WHITE'S BABY WISH*

All available now!

MILLS & BOON®
Hardback – October 2017

ROMANCE

Claimed for the Leonelli Legacy	Lynne Graham
The Italian's Pregnant Prisoner	Maisey Yates
Buying His Bride of Convenience	Michelle Smart
The Tycoon's Marriage Deal	Melanie Milburne
Undone by the Billionaire Duke	Caitlin Crews
His Majesty's Temporary Bride	Annie West
Bound by the Millionaire's Ring	Dani Collins
The Virgin's Shock Baby	Heidi Rice
Whisked Away by Her Sicilian Boss	Rebecca Winters
The Sheikh's Pregnant Bride	Jessica Gilmore
A Proposal from the Italian Count	Lucy Gordon
Claiming His Secret Royal Heir	Nina Milne
Sleigh Ride with the Single Dad	Alison Roberts
A Firefighter in Her Stocking	Janice Lynn
A Christmas Miracle	Amy Andrews
Reunited with Her Surgeon Prince	Marion Lennox
Falling for Her Fake Fiancé	Sue MacKay
The Family She's Longed For	Lucy Clark
Billionaire Boss, Holiday Baby	Janice Maynard
Billionaire's Baby Bind	Katherine Garbera

MILLS & BOON®
Large Print – October 2017

ROMANCE

Sold for the Greek's Heir	Lynne Graham
The Prince's Captive Virgin	Maisey Yates
The Secret Sanchez Heir	Cathy Williams
The Prince's Nine-Month Scandal	Caitlin Crews
Her Sinful Secret	Jane Porter
The Drakon Baby Bargain	Tara Pammi
Xenakis's Convenient Bride	Dani Collins
Her Pregnancy Bombshell	Liz Fielding
Married for His Secret Heir	Jennifer Faye
Behind the Billionaire's Guarded Heart	Leah Ashton
A Marriage Worth Saving	Therese Beharrie

HISTORICAL

The Debutante's Daring Proposal	Annie Burrows
The Convenient Felstone Marriage	Jenni Fletcher
An Unexpected Countess	Laurie Benson
Claiming His Highland Bride	Terri Brisbin
Marrying the Rebellious Miss	Bronwyn Scott

MEDICAL

Their One Night Baby	Carol Marinelli
Forbidden to the Playboy Surgeon	Fiona Lowe
A Mother to Make a Family	Emily Forbes
The Nurse's Baby Secret	Janice Lynn
The Boss Who Stole Her Heart	Jennifer Taylor
Reunited by Their Pregnancy Surprise	Louisa Heaton

MILLS & BOON®
Hardback – November 2017

ROMANCE

The Italian's Christmas Secret	Sharon Kendrick
A Diamond for the Sheikh's Mistress	Abby Green
The Sultan Demands His Heir	Maya Blake
Claiming His Scandalous Love-Child	Julia James
Valdez's Bartered Bride	Rachael Thomas
The Greek's Forbidden Princess	Annie West
Kidnapped for the Tycoon's Baby	Louise Fuller
A Night, A Consequence, A Vow	Angela Bissell
Christmas with Her Millionaire Boss	Barbara Wallace
Snowbound with an Heiress	Jennifer Faye
Newborn Under the Christmas Tree	Sophie Pembroke
His Mistletoe Proposal	Christy McKellen
The Spanish Duke's Holiday Proposal	Robin Gianna
The Rescue Doc's Christmas Miracle	Amalie Berlin
Christmas with Her Daredevil Doc	Kate Hardy
Their Pregnancy Gift	Kate Hardy
A Family Made at Christmas	Scarlet Wilson
Their Mistletoe Baby	Karin Baine
The Texan Takes a Wife	Charlene Sands
Twins for the Billionaire	Sarah M. Anderson

MILLS & BOON®
Large Print – November 2017

ROMANCE

The Pregnant Kavakos Bride	Sharon Kendrick
The Billionaire's Secret Princess	Caitlin Crews
Sicilian's Baby of Shame	Carol Marinelli
The Secret Kept from the Greek	Susan Stephens
A Ring to Secure His Crown	Kim Lawrence
Wedding Night with Her Enemy	Melanie Milburne
Salazar's One-Night Heir	Jennifer Hayward
The Mysterious Italian Houseguest	Scarlet Wilson
Bound to Her Greek Billionaire	Rebecca Winters
Their Baby Surprise	Katrina Cudmore
The Marriage of Inconvenience	Nina Singh

HISTORICAL

Ruined by the Reckless Viscount	Sophia James
Cinderella and the Duke	Janice Preston
A Warriner to Rescue Her	Virginia Heath
Forbidden Night with the Warrior	Michelle Willingham
The Foundling Bride	Helen Dickson

MEDICAL

Mummy, Nurse...Duchess?	Kate Hardy
Falling for the Foster Mum	Karin Baine
The Doctor and the Princess	Scarlet Wilson
Miracle for the Neurosurgeon	Lynne Marshall
English Rose for the Sicilian Doc	Annie Claydon
Engaged to the Doctor Sheikh	Meredith Webber

MILLS & BOON®

Why shop at millsandboon.co.uk?

Each year, thousands of romance readers find their perfect read at millsandboon.co.uk. That's because we're passionate about bringing you the very best romantic fiction. Here are some of the advantages of shopping at www.millsandboon.co.uk:

* **Get new books first**—you'll be able to buy your favourite books one month before they hit the shops

* **Get exclusive discounts**—you'll also be able to buy our specially created monthly collections, with up to 50% off the RRP

* **Find your favourite authors**—latest news, interviews and new releases for all your favourite authors and series on our website, plus ideas for what to try next

* **Join in**—once you've bought your favourite books, don't forget to register with us to rate, review and join in the discussions

Visit **www.millsandboon.co.uk**
for all this and more today!